PULP Literature

PULP *Literature*

PULP LITERATURE PRESS

Issue No. 26, Spring 2020

Pulp Literature Press, Publisher; Jennifer Landels, Managing Editor; Mel Anastasiou, Senior Editor; Jessica Fabrizius, Editor; Genevieve Wynand, Acquisitions Editor; Daniel Cowper, Poetry Editor; Emily Osborne, Poetry Editor; Amanda Bidnall, Copy Editor and Graphic Designer; Mary Rykov, Proofreader; Samantha Olson, Assistant Editor; Carol McCauley, First Reader; Kate Landels, Cover Design. For advertising rates, direct inquiries to info@pulpliterature.com.

Cover painting, *Queen of Swords* by Tais Teng. Artwork for 'Double Flush' by Rina Piccolo. All other illustrations by Mel Anastasiou.

Pulp Literature: ISSN 2292-2164 (Print), ISSN 2292-2172 (Digital), Issue No. 26, Spring 2020.

Published quarterly by Pulp Literature Press, 21955 16 Ave, Langley, BC, Canada V2Z 1K5, pulpliterature.com, at $15.00 per copy. Annual subscription $50.00 in Canada, $68.00 in continental USA, $86.00 elsewhere. Printed in Victoria, BC, Canada, by First Choice Books / Victoria Bindery. Copyright © 2020 Pulp Literature Press. All stories and works of art copyright © 2020 their authors as per bylines.

Pulp Literature Press gratefully acknowledges the support of the Canada Council for the Arts.

Pulp Literature is a proud member of the Magazine Association of BC and Magazines Canada.

TABLE OF CONTENTS

FROM THE PULP LIT PULPIT

The Roaring Twenties

The New Roaring Twenties: perhaps you've heard this phrase in recent months as a new decade pushes out the old, and humans — creatures of comparison that we are — look for something familiar. After all, the 1920s were turbulent times similar to our own. Political, social, and technological changes swept through the world like thunder on the heels of chain lightning. Will the 2020s bring similar upheaval?

It's also tempting to frame the 'New Roaring Twenties' as a hopeful proclamation. In the 1920s social progress and revolution flourished, while art took a dramatic shift in terms of tone, style, and inclusivity. None of us were around to remember it personally, but we like to think those aspects of the 1920s echo in *Pulp Literature*'s pages.

As we round the corner into a new decade, we are tempted to look back and make comparisons as well. However, spring seems like a period of anticipation, not retrospection. So here's to a new decade and more great stories ahead!

~ *Jessica Fabrizius*

*I*N THIS ISSUE

The stunning *Queen of Swords* by cover artist **Tais Teng** guards the gates to this issue's brave new worlds and words.

In 'The Bicolour Spiral' by **Matthew Hughes**, the ever-popular Erm Kaslo explores hostile planets, tracks treasure hunters, and seeks stolen fortune. Matt's futuristic Sam Spade leaves no bloodstained stone unturned in this space opera of mystery and murder.

Life itself spirals with being and absence in 'Watershakers' by **Christi Nogle** and 'The Birthday Party' by **Melisa Gregorio** as children witness the ephemeral made real—and the real made memory.

And words themselves whirl and twirl—and crack open secrets—as poets **Patti Pangborn** and **Sarah Summerson** explore the hidden spaces of family life.

Mike Carson, runner-up for the SiWC Storyteller Award, continues the exploration of memory and family in 'Deep Water', considering the limits of responsibility in fragile relationships.

Meanwhile, **Rina Piccolo**, in 'Double Flush', reminds us that being human sometimes just means looking out for number one.

It's buyer beware in 'Life4Sale', an epistolary tale for the digital age by Raven Short Story Contest winner **Michael Donoghue**. And threads of desire and longing stitch lives together in 'Dannemora Sewing Class' by runner-up **MFC Feeley**.

Two historical heroines return as we rejoin Toinette — 'La Bergere' — at the gates of seventeenth-century Paris in part two of *The Shepherdess* by **JM Landels**, and Frankie Ray and her chum Connie brave the no-less-imposing gates of Monument Studios in part four of **Mel Anastasiou's** *The Extra*.

Abandon the humdrum and enter these realms of wonder and adventure if you dare ...

Jes, Gen, Mel, Jen & Sam
Pulp Literature Press

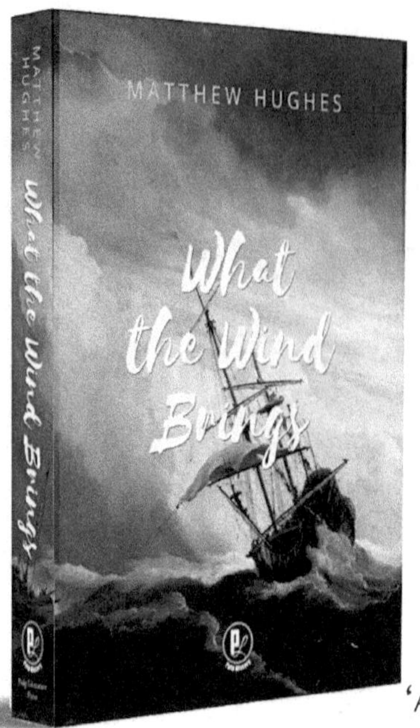

Out of the fires of a Caribbean slave revolt, shipwrecked on the jungle coast of 16th-century Ecuador, an educated slave, a shaman, and a monk hunted by the Inquisition fight for freedom against the might of Imperial Spain.

Dive into an epic slipstream novel of intrigue and adventure from fantasy author Matthew Hughes, the writer George R.R. Martin calls 'criminally underrated,' and Robert J. Sawyer says is 'a towering talent.'

'A triumph!' - Cecelia Holland
'Sensational' - Candas Jane Dorsey

pulpliterature.com

Fantastic Fresh Fiction!

PULP *Literature*

THE BICOLOUR SPIRAL

Matthew Hughes

Matthew Hughes writes in many genres under many names, including Matt Hughes and Hugh Matthews. He has won the Arthur Ellis Award from the Crime Writers of Canada and has been short-listed for the Aurora, Nebula, Philip K Dick, Endeavour (twice), AE van Vogt, and Derringer Awards. Now he has pulled out all the stops for a foray into historical fiction, and we are thrilled to be his publisher for this endeavour. His magnum opus, What the Wind Brings, is available now through our website: pulpliterature.com/product-category/novels/matthew-hughes/. You can follow Matt on his Patreon page for updates.

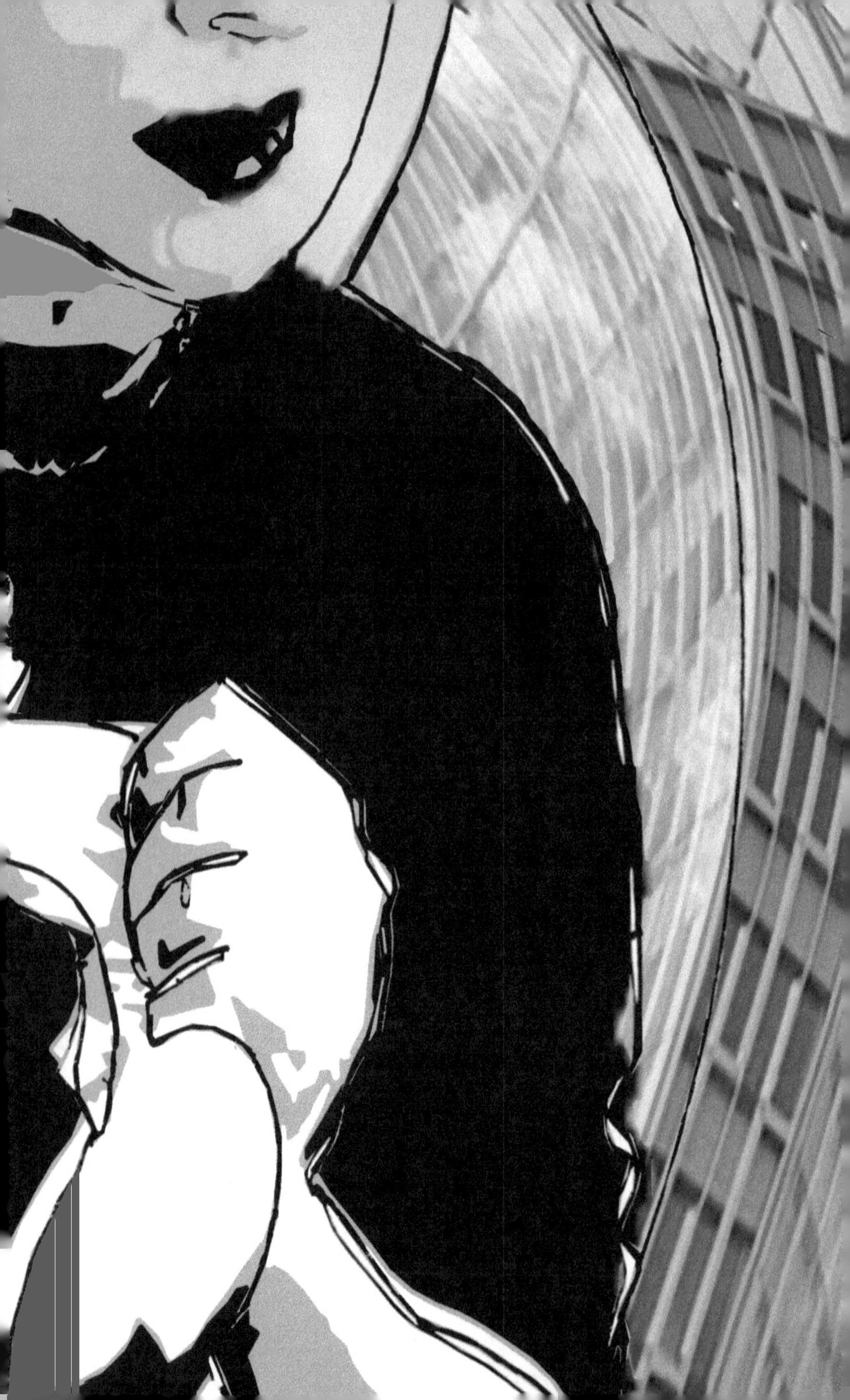

The Bicolour Spiral

The young woman was nervous, wringing her soft cap between two pale hands, her gaze moving from place to place in Erm Kaslo's workroom because she was unable—or at least not yet ready—to meet the confidential operative's assessing stare.

"Sit down," Kaslo said. "Take a breath. I haven't bitten anybody … in ages."

The remark did not win him a smile. The visitor lowered herself into a chair then scooted forward until her narrow buttocks were perched on the edge of the cushion.

"It's a comfy chair," the op said, taking a position on the corner of his work table and adopting what was meant to be a reassuring tone. "People who come to see me professionally are often under considerable strain. I try to encourage them to relax."

The young woman looked up at him, then quickly away. Her hands continued to worry the hat.

"A mug of punge?" Kaslo said. "Or a drop of something stronger?"

A sharp shake of the head caused a lock of lank blonde hair to fall in her face. She brushed it aside and went back to work on the cap.

Kaslo suppressed a sigh. He said, "How about we start with you telling me your name?"

It took two attempts, the first strangled by a dry throat. Finally, the young woman managed to say, "Kundlemaz. Purindath Kundlemaz."

Kaslo's encouraging expression did not change, but he recognized the name. Murderers were rare on the long-settled world of Novo Bantry, even here in its capital, which called itself 'The City of the Crystal Towers', though its more prosaic name was the Commune of Indoberia.

"And why have you come to consult me?" he said, though he knew the answer.

"I ..." The cap took more punishment. "It's ..."

Kaslo changed tack. "It's because the Provost's Department intends to arrest you. For the murder of your uncle. They're just waiting for the warrant to arrive from ... where is it again?"

The already pale face before him had now gone ashen. Kundlemaz half rose from the chair, her eyes wide and panicky now, her head turning to make sure she knew where the door was.

The op slid off the desk and laid a firm but gentle hand on the woman's shoulder, which trembled like some small and defenceless creature that knows it is being hunted.

"It's all right," Kaslo said. "You've come to the right place. They won't arrest you if you engage me."

"Is that really true?" said Kundlemaz, a faint light of hope diluting the fear in her face. "I mean, I'd heard ... but I didn't know."

"How would you? You've never been accused of a crime before, have you?" Kaslo didn't need to ask. The look of a potential client told him all he needed to know. Crime was rare on Novo Bantry, where life was easy and the human mind well ordered.

Passions seldom boiled over, and, in the rare incidences when emotions ran amok, the cause could usually be traced to a malfunctioning of the brain resulting from physiological disorder or overindulgence in powerful stimulants.

Purindath Kundlemaz showed no signs of either. She looked like a young woman whose hitherto smooth voyage across the ocean of enjoyable existence had suddenly been wrecked on uncharted rocks. Kaslo patted the air in a quieting gesture and said, "If you engage me — and I accept the assignment — I will stand surety for you until your case is heard by the arbiters. You will not be confined, and I will be responsible for you."

Kundlemaz settled back into the chair, blinking and nodding as she took this in. Then Kaslo saw the fear come back. "I don't know," the young woman said, "if I can afford you."

"Your uncle was a wealthy man," the op said. "You are his sole heir, if what the Provost's Department says is accurate. You should have no trouble paying my fee."

"If I am convicted, I cannot inherit. It will all go to the Commune."

Kaslo smiled. "All the more reason I should work hard in your behalf." He went to the confectionary and had it generate two mugs of hot, steaming punge. He gave one to Kundlemaz, who let her cap fall into her lap. Her hands had lost the worst of their tremors.

The op sat in his work chair, took a sip of the brew, and said, "Now, take a good long drink and tell me what you know."

Kaslo had heard the story the day before from one of his contacts within the Indoberia Provost's Department: Sub-Inspector Fourna Houdibras, a senior provost with whom Kaslo had a long-standing relationship, had informed him of the forthcoming extradition request. It had arrived from the Wardens Force on the secondary world of Fancheree farther down The Spray. Now, as he listened to Kundlemaz give her rendition, he was alert to any points that differed from the official account.

The young woman's uncle, Lutz Kundlemaz, had been a wealthy magnate of Indoberia. His fortune derived from his ownership of several well-functioning enterprises and his social status from a number of eleemosynary donations to worthy causes. The elder man's passion, however, was his collection of Erythreotic pearls, of which he had several dozen, including the only known bicolour anyone had ever discovered. Its value was beyond price, and Lutz Kundlemaz was known to have turned down an offer of an entire world — small and somewhat remote, to be sure, but an eminently habitable place with a sparse population who were agreeable to letting someone else see to all the necessities of managing a planet.

At the mention of the Erythreotic bicolour, Kaslo interrupted. "Describe it to me."

Purindath Kundlemaz held out a not very large fist. "A sphere a little smaller than that," she said, "with two swirling spirals of cream and ochre, the edges of each quite distinct from the other."

Kaslo watched as Purindath described the precious object that drove true collectors into paroxysms and trances. He saw none of that fetishism in the young woman's countenance and let the story continue.

"I received a message," Purindath said, "that a new trove of pearls had been discovered. I told my uncle—"

Kaslo interrupted. "How was the message conveyed? By your integrator?"

"No," said the young woman, and Kaslo watched closely as the next words came. He was trained in interrogation and was able to read micro-expressions as they flashed across an interviewee's features. Later, he could have his integrator replay these seconds at a speed that would reveal all, but his impression now was that Purindath was telling the truth as she knew it.

"A man came to the door, an old space-hand by the whiteness of his hair and the shape of his ear clips. He told me that he was off a tramp freighter that had stopped at a world called Erythreot, where he was approached by a man who gave him a sealed envelope and a credit chip. As soon as my uncle's integrator validated the chip, he was to turn over the message."

"To your uncle, or to either of you?" Kaslo said.

"Either."

"And your integrator validated the chip?"

"Yes. It was a cash voucher, redeemable at any fiduciary pool."

That could be checked, Kaslo knew, and it would be. But credit chips circulated throughout the Ten Thousand Worlds and were not traceable, to the delight of thieves and fences up and down The Spray.

He waited while Purindath finished her punge and handed back the mug. The young woman seemed more settled now. "Go on," Kaslo said.

"I told my uncle when he returned from his meeting. He opened the envelope and read the message. It was from a man who described himself as a prospector and who said he had discovered a trove of pearls in a chest on the Plain of Baderoth. He was sending this discreet communication to the most prominent collector of Erythreotic pearls, knowing that my uncle would pay the best price in any auction but that a private sale would mean letting the seller out of having to pay commission to the auctioneer."

"Plausible," said Kaslo. The remark won him a sharp look from Purindath, which was the op's intent. Again, he saw a genuine expression: the annoyance of someone who tells the truth and sees a sceptical reception.

"Then what?" he said.

The next element of the young woman's story tallied with the Provost's Department's information. Lutz Kundlemaz had immediately told his integrator to lease a space yacht. Within an hour, he and his niece were lifting off from the south side of Indoberia's spaceport and heading for the whimsy that would fling them through nonspace and discharge the ship within a half day's passage through normal space to Erythreot.

The spacer's message had specified a set of coordinates, and they touched down at the landing pad of one of the ghost towns that speckled the barren wasteland. They stepped out onto an endless expanse of pebbles and grit, mostly flat but with low hills that looked, as they made their descent through the thin atmosphere, like ripples on a beach.

"The instructions said to walk east, climb a slight rise, then look on the other side for 'something out of the ordinary'," Purindath said. "And to come alone. My uncle went."

"No integrator?"

"The message said not to."

"Was he armed?"

Purindath signalled an assent. "His energy pistol."

"Self-aiming?"

"No, he prided himself on his facility with the weapon."

Kaslo made a noncommittal sound and said, "Then what?"

"I waited. My uncle said that he expected we would find another message that would lead him to the next stage of the journey."

"He didn't think it might be a hoax?"

"He admitted of the possibility," the young woman said. "But the prospect of adding to his collection outweighed the chance of being made to look like a fool."

"So he expected he would go over the rise and soon return. But he didn't."

The hat took more punishment. "No, and after a while I began to worry. When more time passed, my anxiety deepened. I told the ship to rise up and use its percepts to scan the area."

"And you saw your uncle?"

"Yes. He was on the other side of the hill, next to a cairn of rocks, lying face down."

Purindath had set the yacht down nearby and run to help her uncle. But Lutz Kundlemaz was beyond all aid. Someone had smashed in the back of his head. A gore-stained pebble lay beside the corpse. The energy pistol was still in its holster. And there was no one in sight in any direction.

The niece had used the ship's cargo loader to transfer the body into the hold, then bade the vessel's integrator to contact the planet's connectivity grid. She was surprised to discover that Erythreot did not have one. The ship had to revert to a primitive broadcast method. Purindath found herself talking to a man who identified himself as a community vigilo in a town some distance away. The man said he would have to send a message by outbound ship to the secondary world, Fancheree, whose Wardens handled criminal offenses beyond the vigilos' capacity.

"He told me to stay where I was. When I asked how long, he said it might take several days for a cruiser to arrive from Fancheree. If I left, I would probably be considered a fugitive."

"But you did leave."

"I was alone in a desert with a murderer," the young woman said.

"You had an energy pistol."

"So had my uncle. It did not help him."

"So," Kaslo said, "you came back to Novo Bantry and reported the homicide to the Provost's Department."

"Yes. They took charge of my uncle's body, put this on me" — she pulled down the collar of her upper garment to show a torc around her neck — "and told me to wait while they dealt with the Fancheree Wardens Force."

And now Fancheree wanted her. Kaslo was not familiar with the world. He spoke to his integrator. "What is the attitude on Fancheree towards transgression?"

"Theirs is a stern culture," said the device, "based on the doctrine of Liberative Piacularity."

"Ah," said Kaslo, nodding. The philosophy was active on a number of planets. Sinners were relieved of their guilt by being relieved of their corporeal existence. It was a lengthy and exacting process.

It appeared from Purindath Kundlemaz's expression that she had already researched Liberative Piacularity.

"I will take the case," Kaslo said.

Lutz Kundlemaz had leased the yacht for a Novo Bantry month, and Kaslo was able to use it for the remainder of the period. That saved time in getting to Erythreot, since the remote world was far off any of the routes taken by passenger lines. Even

Fancheree, a long-settled secondary, was otherwise reachable only by freighters that deigned to carry a few passengers.

Thus it was only three days after their interview on Novo Bantry that the yacht's integrator informed Kaslo that they were decelerating towards the planet. Kaslo told it to set down at the same coordinates the murdered man had specified.

During the voyage, the op had consulted *Hobey's Guide to the Minor and Disregarded Planets* and learned what there was to be learned about Erythreot and its long-extinct species. The world was a little smaller than most settled planets, but it could barely be called habitable. It circled a nondescript yellow star at the right distance for living creatures to have formed and flourished, and it appeared that its shallow seas had produced not only sentient life but at least one species that qualified as sapient.

The extent of the vanished Erythreots' development was unknown, though it was obvious that their civilization had not reached a level that allowed them to leave their world and find refuge on other planets. That was their tragedy, because long before humanity had even reached the stage of banging rocks together, Erythreot became an unhappy venue for life.

The problem was the yellow star, named Habbash according to *Hobey's*. Roughly a million years ago, its internal dynamics caused a spate of instability that lasted some tens of thousands of years. In simple terms, Habbash flickered. When it was bright, its greater warmth caused much of Erythreot's water to rise and thicken the atmosphere. When it was dim, it caused the moisture to fall as snow that never melted, covering the planet in a mantle of ice.

Habbash would alternate its output every few hundred years, creating an ebb and flow of glaciers across the world's surface. The first global ice-encasement ended the existence of the Erythreots, first freezing them in their subaqueous haunts, then grinding them and all their works to gravel as the ice sheets came and went. Indeed, the entire surface of Erythreot was so comprehensively scoured, over the fifty thousand or more years of intermittent ice ages, that the world was almost uniformly covered by sand and pebbles, and a rock larger than a man's head was a rarity. In most places, the water table was so high that footprints filled up in moments.

No trace of the Erythreots' civilization survived except for a few deep mines and some graves that had been laid in abyssal sea chasms. These depressions were found by the first prospectors to visit the planet. They came seeking rare mineral compounds — there were none, but their exploratory drillings turned up fossilized fragments of the ultraterrenes themselves and the strange orbs the first finders had called pearls. Now a handful of prospectors searched for more of the smooth, opaque objects, but a new find was rare.

No one knew what role the pearls might have played in the lives of Erythreots, only that they accompanied them in death. Whatever sea creature had formed them had been crushed and eroded into oblivion, along with every other form of life on the planet above the microscopic. All that was known was that the pearls were objects of supernal beauty, and no more than a few hundred existed in public and private connoissariums up and down The Spray.

The pearls rarely came onto the market, usually only when an aficionado died. A newly discovered cemetery, even a single grave, was bound to draw intense interest from collectors — and any of them would pay a fortune to own a virgin pearl. The whispered possibility of such a find would cause enthusiasts to drop every other concern and rush to Erythreot. A direct and secret summons had brought Lutz Kundlemaz there as soon as he could lease a yacht.

"Did Kundlemaz have you scan the landing area?" Kaslo said as the ship sank through the planet's atmosphere.

"Yes. I saw nothing untoward," said the ship.

"Do so now."

"Still nothing."

When the yacht was in the last minute of its descent, Kaslo bade it stop and hover. He had brought with him his travelling valise, which contained the core of the integrator that served as his assistant and could perform a number of sophisticated functions. He now took the innocuous-seeming bag to the forward hatch and told the ship to open.

The upper air flooded in, dank and cold. Kaslo's valise extended a number of percepts and sensors. After a moment, it said, "No one there. No sentient devices. No traps."

"Traces?" the op said.

A screen appeared above the bag and filled with an image of a stony slope and a rough pyramid of stones that the scale at the bottom of the screen showed to be approximately waist-high. A faint trail of footprints, rendered in wanly glowing green, approached the cairn.

"Kundlemaz approached from the west, reached the cairn, and stood there long enough for his weight to make the stones settle beneath him," the valise said. "Something drew his attention. While he was so occupied, a shielded air car came from the north. The occupant did not get out of the vehicle but struck the victim from behind. The vehicle then departed to the south."

"Can you track it?"

The scale of the screen's image increased so that Kaslo was now looking at a wide sweep of territory. A faint blue line indicated the path of the killer's air car. His assistant said, "It rose as it travelled. Eventually it stopped, and the emanations of its gravity obviators ceased."

"Since it didn't plummet to the ground," Kaslo said, "it must have met a spaceship and been taken aboard."

"Most likely."

"Land near the cairn. We'll take a closer look."

Kaslo waited while his assistant made an intense scan of the piled stones and the surrounding area. He didn't need it to identify the murder weapon: the gore-stained rock lay next to where a pool of blood had drained into the pebbled ground. His integrator told him that no traces of the assailant remained on the weapon.

"But there is this," it said, and shone a beam of light at a spot near the top of the cairn.

Kaslo approached, lifted a rock, and found beneath it a small triangular scrap of paper with two sides at right angles to each other and the third a jagged tear.

"The corner of a sheet of paper," he said.

"Very common stuff," his assistant said. "Not traceable. The message it contained might be, but there is no sign of it."

"So," Kaslo said, "Kundlemaz approaches as specified, finds a note, and pulls it free of the rock that holds it down. As he is reading it, the screened air car—probably a ship's utility car-ryall—glides silently up behind him. The killer strikes him down, retrieves the paper, and departs."

"All we can do is try to identify the ship," said the valise.

"On a planet without a connectivity grid, there may be no record of its coming and going. It could have come from anywhere and gone anywhere."

"Perhaps," said his assistant, "the person in the air car now descending rapidly toward us from the northeast will be able to shed some light."

Kaslo looked in that direction and saw a dark dot in the sky. It was enlarging quickly as it angled down toward him.

"It is unlikely to be a coincidence," he said. "Withdraw your sensors and be ready to act at the usual signal. Or if I become incapacitated."

It was a good sign that the vehicle was visible, but an ambiguous one that it bore on its blunt nose an official insignia. The same device — a pattern of keys and chains — was displayed on the badge that its occupant wore on a sash that went over one shoulder and connected to a belt that supported several pouches and the holster of a compact disorganizer. The vehicle's operator drew the weapon as the air car landed at an actionable distance between Kaslo and the space yacht.

Kaslo put his hands where they could be seen. He studied the large, square-jawed specimen who stepped out of the vehicle, the weapon pointed at the ground between them — though aimed more toward the op than toward its wielder's feet. The man's gaze flicked here, there, rested on the valise for a moment, then came back to the op. Kaslo had often seen police agents assessing a scene and knew he was witnessing the procedure once again.

"Do I need to disable that?" the man said, with a nod of his head toward the valise.

"Not from my point of view," said Kaslo. "I would like to show you my credentials."

The man touched a pouch on the front of his belt and said, "I have already seen them. My assistant is checking them now."

"You are not of the local vigilo, then."

"Detainer, Third Degree, Frobe Mundun," said the other. "Fancheree Wardens Force."

Kaslo smiled. "You have been waiting for the culprit to return to the scene of the crime?"

"It happens sometimes," Mundun said, but then he nodded at some new information only he was receiving and holstered his weapon. "My ship"—his hand moved to indicate the sky above them—"has identified you."

"But there is no connectivity here," Kaslo said.

Mundun explained: the Wardens had anticipated that Purindath Kundlemaz would engage a confidential operative to examine the scene, and could afford a serious practitioner. A list of those based on Novo Bantry had been prepared. "You were high on the list," he said.

"Highest, I should hope," said Kaslo. The other man shrugged, and the op changed the subject. "Shall we pool?"

"I think we should," said the Warden. "You go first."

A short while later, they were in the yacht's salon. Mundun had not eaten for many hours while he had been watching Kaslo approach and land, and the leased ship's kitchen was superior to what was offered by the Wardens Force cruiser. As was proper, they engaged in inconsequential talk over ship's bread and a selection of small dishes that ranged from piquant to savoury, washed down with steaming mugs of punge. The op spoke of Indoberia's many admirable qualities. The detainer revealed himself to be an enthusiastic adherent of Fancheree's dominant philosophy; Kaslo learned some startling and lurid details about Liberative Piacularity.

Finally, when both were satisfied, Kaslo bid the ship's integrator to withdraw the table and told his assistant to produce the evidence. Mundun studied the screen and said, "Your device sifts more finely than ours. We can detect the traces the shielded air car's obviators left while it was standing still near the cairn, but we lose the trail once it begins to climb through thinner air."

"It was camouflage of a very high order," Kaslo said, "custom designed and calibrated to as fine a degree as we're likely to see."

Mundun noted that such systems are usually available only to police agencies on the most developed of the Ten Thousand Worlds, or to extremely well-funded criminals.

"That contrasts with the simplicity of the killing itself," Kaslo said. "A local rock smashed against the head might argue for a lack of familiarity with sophisticated weapons."

"Self-aiming weapons can be interrogated," said the Warden, "even if efforts have been made to erase their records. A rock has little to say."

Mundun returned his attention to the screen and traced the faint blue line up into the limits of the atmosphere. "Another ship," he said. "A yacht like this one?"

"Too easily traceable," said Kaslo, "whether hired or privately owned. I assume you will have consulted records of any recent traffic."

Mundun signalled assent. "Not much comes this way. There is one whimsy — the one you came through — that brings traffic from up The Spray, and another that connects us to Fancheree." He drained his mug of punge and said the only recent traffic through The Spray had been the two trips made by the yacht they were sitting in. The whimsy for ships heading to and from his world had carried the regular packet between Erythreot and Fancheree, and a few tramp freighters.

"The packet would not have a shielded utility vehicle," said Kaslo, "and, even if it did, it would not let a passenger use the vehicle."

"No," said the Warden. "So we're looking at freighters."

"Have you done so already?"

"On a cursory basis," said Mundun. "Now we will dig — once we have returned to a world that has a connectivity to dig through." He tapped his fingers on his empty mug in a thoughtful rhythm and continued, "I think we can withdraw the extradition request."

When the elements of a case began to fit themselves together in Kaslo's mind, his eyes often took on a dreamy look. They did that now. After a moment he said, "You could, but I suggest you don't."

The yacht took them to Fancheree, where Kaslo's assistant connected to the Wardens Force's system. He and Mundun began to sift through the records of the freighters that had come and gone through the whimsy between Fancheree and Erythreot.

"These," Mundun said, pointing to three of the vessels noted on the screen that hung before them, "pass this way almost often enough to be considered regular visitors." Now he indicated a fourth, a tramp freighter named *Shangalang*. "That one has come and gone but once."

The Wardens' integrator interrogated the controller at the spaceport where the singled-out ship had stopped. It reported, "This *Shangalang* took on no cargo. It stopped only for repairs."

"What kind of repairs?" Kaslo asked.

"Its integrator was displaying . . . inconsistencies." The Wardens' integrator used the euphemism that sentient devices employed when discussing delicate matters touching upon the reliability of integrators. Aging systems, if their parameters were not occasionally recalibrated, could develop a condition known as 'the vagues'. In the case of a domestic integrator charged with running a household, the disorder might result in a dinner being undercooked or a lumen left burning all night. A spaceship with the vagues might inadvertently open all the airlocks, causing everyone on board to be sucked out into space.

"Did the freighter come into port under its integrator's guidance?" Kaslo asked.

"No," was the answer from the port. "Its captain brought it into dock manually. Its integrator was disengaged."

The op continued, "But the ship's integrator, once restored to full efficiency, took the ship out again?"

"Yes."

Kaslo looked at Mundun. "We need to know more about the *Shangalang*."

"Indeed," said the detainer. "Integrator, show us what we have on the crew."

Several images appeared, head-and-shoulders renderings of the seven-person crew, each accompanied by job title and biographical information. Kaslo studied the images for a moment before focusing on the freighter's captain. To his own assistant, he said, "Display the image of the spacer who brought the message to Lutz Kundlemaz's house."

His integrator put up the image that had been captured by the who's-there at Kundlemaz's front door. Skin and eye colour had been changed and efforts made to alter the shape of the nose and hairline, but the two images were of the same man.

"Gruen Podesko," Kaslo read from the port's display. "I doubt we'll find him under that name. Nor will the *Shangalang* show up under any searches, I'll wager."

And so it proved to be. Messages were sent out to the nearest Grand Foundational Domains, the worlds settled in ancient times when humanity made the first Great Effloration into The Spray. The messages had to go by ship because there could be no interconnectivity through whimsies. But a homicide was a sufficiently grave matter for the Wardens Force to send couriers, and the responses were back within a couple of days.

"There are seventeen Gruen Podeskos listed among the several dozen worlds in this sector of The Spray," Mundun reported. "None can be our captain. As well, there is no ship registered as the *Shangalang*, although a freighter of that name was broken up at a shipyard on Caletho two years ago."

"The pieces fall into place," said Kaslo. "Whatever the *Shangalang*'s real name may be, its integrator core was removed while it was en route to Fancheree. This Podesko brought it in manually. Then he used your port's services to revive the core of the dead ship, at least enough to take it out of range of your connectivity, leaving a false record. Once clear of detection, he would have reinstalled the proper core."

The detainer agreed. "The ship went to Novo Bantry, where the captain delivered the message to the victim. It then travelled to Erythreot, where he built the cairn and waited for Kundlemaz to come and be killed."

"The question now," Kaslo said, "is whether this Podesko is the prime mover behind the scheme or just a paid hireling."

"If a hireling, a well-paid one," Mundun suggested. "He will probably have taken his anonymous ship to a distant sector, sold it for scrap, and retired."

"What about the crew?" Kaslo posed the question and answered it himself. "The fewer who know, the safer for Podesko. And no need to share."

"Hard to kill six people in the confines of a spaceship without risk," the Warden said. "He'd have to get them all at once. Try it one at a time, and somebody might notice and resist."

The op thought for a moment then said, "He could have parked the ship above Erythreot, taken out the core again on the pretext of its needing more calibration. He takes it with him down to the surface, leaving the crew without percepts, then returns after killing Kundlemaz, restores the integrator, and speeds away to collect his fee. At the next port, he discharges the crew, who know nothing and can therefore reveal nothing."

"Feasible," said Mundun. "Now how do we catch him?"

"And," Kaslo said, "the one who hired him."

Purindath Kundlemaz's extradition to Fancheree caused a considerable stir in the Commune of Indoberia, where the young woman was known to many of the social elite. It was rumoured that the evidence against her was incontrovertible.

Another brouhaha ensued when news came, only weeks later, that Purindath had been convicted and had faced the ultimate sanction under Fancheree's starkly efficient system of Liberative Piacularity. Young Kundlemaz was reported to have been freed of all further responsibility for her existence, with her ashes scattered, as customary on Fancheree, to the ceaseless winds that blew across the Karhoff Escarpment.

Her uncle's estate, there being no other heirs, was consigned to the Commune, which announced a series of auctions. The first of these, the forthcoming sale of the decedent's famed collection of Erythreotic pearls, was made known to collectors far up and down The Spray, and ample time was allowed for them to make arrangements to be there.

Attended by a strong presence from the Provost's Department, the event was convened in what had been the dancing chamber of Lutz Kundlemaz's house-in-town. Sixty plush chairs were set out in a demilune in front of the proscenium-arched bandstand, and all were filled, with a hundred more bidders standing to the rear and the sides. Drawn from scores of worlds, the crowd displayed an unending variety of clothing, skin paints, hats and hairstyles, ornaments and baubles.

Grod Ors, the owner of Indoberia's pre-eminent firm of auctioneers, presided. He leaned on a cane of gnarled and twisted wyrhwood, which he rapped smartly on the bandstand's floor to announce the opening of the sale. A hush fell over the high-ceilinged chamber as the first lot was brought out: half a dozen pale ordinaries, the kind found in the graves of juvenile Erythreots.

Bidding was brisk, and Ors soon struck the floor to signal that the ordinaries would go to a dealer from a world down The Spray. The next lot was brought out—three pearls of a higher quality—and the auction resumed. In less than an hour, the bulk of the Kundlemaz collection was disposed of, including some ultra high-grade specimens that sold for more than Kaslo, though he was well paid, earned in a decade.

Then came the crowning moment. To a chorus of gasps and whispers, a pair of Grod Ors's mature sons brought forth the gold-and-crystal case that contained the bicolour spiral. Set in an armature that was draped in cloth of an electric blue, the pearl seemed to hang in space, weightless, complete, and perfect.

When the room fell again into silence, Ors said he would entertain a first bid of ten million sovereign debt units. Immediately a hand rose from the middle of the chairs.

"Twenty million SDUs," said the old auctioneer, and saw a raised finger make a circle near the front. He took note and said, "Thirty million."

And so it proceeded. At first, there were a dozen bidders, but as the numbers rose beyond three hundred million SDUs, the less-endowed hopefuls fell away. At five hundred million there were four contenders; at seven hundred million only three remained. And as the bids neared a billion SDUs, there were only two competitors left: a Lord Algrove, a first-tier aristocrat from Old Earth, a fusty little world farther up The Spray (it was he who had once offered the dead man an entire planet for the bicolour spiral); and Irczy Ferranian, Novo Bantry's foremost shipping magnate, who had already acquired several of the prime lots. Kaslo did not know the Old Earther, but had brushed up against Ferranian a few years back, when the op had helped break up an interworld smuggling ring.

The bids were now rising in increments of fifty million SDUs, the old man leaning on his cane as he noted each offer with only the slightest motion of his almost hairless head. Finally, as the billion mark was passed, Irczy Ferranian stood and threw back the long, trailing sleeves of his upper garment, revealing the sparkle of rings and bracelets that adorned his fingers and wrists. In a voice as calm as if he were discussing the weather, he said, "One billion, five hundred million."

Now the hushed room heard a collective intake of breath. Irczy Ferranian did not bother to glance at Lord Algrove but sat down again and calmly inspected his nails. Up on the bandstand, Grod Ors repeated the number, waited a long moment, then repeated it again. When the silence continued, he said, "Selling at one billion, five hundred million SDUs."

He let the figure hang in the air then struck the floor with the ferrule of his cane and said, "Sold."

The auction was a temporary wonder in Indoberia. Within a few days, some new sensation had come to lay hold of popular attention. Time passed. Lutz Kundlemaz's house-in-town stood dark and shuttered, awaiting the Commune's decision to put it on the market. His unfortunate niece, Purindath, was rarely spoken of.

Irczy Ferranian had several homes but kept his Erythreotic pearls collection at his country estate, a twenty-minute flight from Indoberia. After the auction, Kaslo moved into a cottage not far from the estate's eastern boundary. He made certain preparations, then settled to wait.

Twenty-four days after the auction, the op had his assistant contact Sub-Inspector Fourna Houdibras. "Are we on?" said the provost, when she answered the call.

"We are," said Kaslo. "I am going in now and would appreciate it if you could alert the local detachment."

"Doing so now," said Houdibras. "I'll be with you as soon as possible."

Kaslo regarded the image on the screen hanging in the air before him: a faint blue line descending from above the atmosphere and angling down towards a patch of forest not far from the northern edge of Ferranian's estate. "Any indication he has noticed our surveillance?" he asked the integrator.

"We have assumed the target has investigated Ferranian's wards and watchers and adjusted his camouflage to tickle his way past them," said the integrator. "Whereas our percepts are calibrated out of phase with the target's. If he adjusted his percepts to look across our frequencies, he would alert the estate's defences."

"That would be no, then," said Kaslo.

"It would and is," said his assistant, causing the op to make a mental note to strip down the device for a rebuild as soon as this case was concluded.

He carried the valise out to his volante and had it mesh with the vehicle's systems. He then bade it deploy a camouflaging shield set to the same standards as the one the vehicle descending from orbit was using. Now, almost entirely invisible to the estate's senses, he told the air car to plot a vector to intercept the descending vehicle.

The volante's obviators were silent as it rose and proceeded past the northeast corner of the estate. "All seems to be in order," his assistant volunteered. "The estate integrator's percepts should see us as a moth drifting in over the eastern wall. The target vehicle will have the same profile."

"Then we will be a pair of moths. Get behind it when it crosses the wall."

Kaslo's volante inched toward the barrier. "Here he comes," said his assistant. The op felt a slight vibration irritate his teeth and cranial bones as the target vehicle passed overhead and he was temporarily bathed in the downflux of its obviators. Then the sensation faded and he said, "Follow him in."

Kaslo's air car glided forward. His integrator adjusted its percepts, and now the vehicle in front became barely visible, a pale, translucent object in the shape of a ship's utility carryall. It slid gently down to land on the forecourt of the manse's ceremonial entrance. Its canopy rose, and out stepped a ghostly figure.

"Elision suit," his assistant said, "as expected."

"Cut the babble," Kaslo said. He pulled up the cowl and face mask of his own elision suit, a garment whose nanotube-covered exterior captured photons and other electromagnetic energies, bending them around the wearer. He judged that the intruder's suit was as high-grade as his own.

The other man did not go toward the tall carved doors atop the wide steps but slanted toward a small portal to the side of the stairs. Meanwhile, Kaslo's air car had come to a silent stop behind the shielded carryall.

"Once we're in," Kaslo said, "disable that."

"Okey doke," said his assistant.

The intruder had no trouble with whatever defences guarded the door. It was as Kaslo had expected: the man had been here before. The op moved quickly and silently after him, passing the door's who's-there unnoticed and entering the manse almost on the fellow's heels.

Without his assistant's enhanced percepts to scan the space in front of the op, the figure in the elision suit was invisible. But even high-grade e-suits could not completely disguise the effect of a human foot pressing down on a parquet floor: the tiny and temporary rise in temperature that the pressure evoked in the polished wood. Kaslo focused on the floor before him and saw the faint foot-shadows appear and fade. He followed.

Besides, he knew where the man was going. He had studied the plans of Irczy Ferranian's great house and knew where the plutocrat was most likely to be at this time of night — as, apparently, did the intruder.

So he silently followed the invisible man through corridors that connected the subterranean chambers of the manse, where Ferranian's few human servants operated and where they stored all the delicacies and bonbons that made the shipping magnate's life such a rare feast.

They passed two staircases and an ascender tube, then the footprints paused at the foot of a third flight of stairs. Kaslo froze, listening. After a moment, he saw a pale shadow of a sole appear on the bottom step, then another on the next riser. The op moved forward and climbed.

The staircase bent to the left, spiralling upward. Kaslo went softly, watching the footshadows appear and fade. Then they stopped and stayed. A moment later, there came a soft click, and the stairwell was flooded with light as the man ahead opened a narrow door and stepped out into a brightly lit room.

Kaslo followed quickly, but the intruder did not bother to close the door. The op went through and found himself in a vault-ceilinged chamber plushly furnished in the gold and crimson currently fashionable at the top of Indoberia's social pyramid.

Irczy Ferranian, seated at an ornate table, had looked up, mildly surprised, as the door opened. Kaslo passed through it just in time to see surprise become angry suspicion. The magnate's mouth opened to address the house's integrator, but the intruder moved fast, and the op saw Ferranian's lips flattened by the pressure of an invisible hand. At the same time, a white mark appeared on the man's forehead, which Kaslo identified as the shape of an energy pistol's emitter.

A harsh voice whispered. "The weapon is sentient. It will discharge if you make an untoward sound. Understood?"

The unseen hand left Ferranian's mouth. "Yes," he said.

"You spoke?" said the house integrator, its voice sounding from the air.

"Disengage yourself," said Ferranian. "Maintain only minimal functions until I say otherwise."

The device said it would comply.

The hard voice said, "That better not be a code for 'Call the provosts'. This is all or nothing for me."

"It isn't," Ferranian said. "Now take the damn mask off, Boronet. I don't like conversing with ghosts."

A lean hard face appeared, then the rest of the head, topped by a shock of white hair that identified Boronet as a veteran spacer. The head appeared to float in the air, looking down at Ferranian, who glowered up at it.

"I suppose you've come to blackmail me," the plutocrat said. He folded his arms across his chest. "I've paid you enough."

"No," said Captain Boronet, slowly shaking his head.

Kaslo could hear the magnate's teeth grinding. "I won't let you bleed me!"

The disembodied head laughed. "I mean, no, I haven't come to blackmail you."

Confusion now appeared on Ferranian's face. "I don't understand."

"It should be obvious," said the spacer. He slipped off the elision cloth that covered the pistol and used the weapon to gesture briefly toward the object that rested in the centre of the polished table top, the object Irczy Ferranian had been delighting in when the narrow door had opened.

Comprehension dawned, and the magnate reached for the spiral bicolour Erythreotic pearl. "No!" he cried.

The pistol came around to point once more at Ferranian's head. The spacer said, "I had nothing against Lutz Kundlemaz, but I killed him for it. I have never liked you. I won't mind killing you at all."

That's all I need, Kaslo told himself. He stepped forward and placed his hands around the spacer's neck. Elision suits were not protection against expertly sited and applied pressure. The pistol fell from the killer's nerveless grip. Kaslo let the man follow the weapon to the floor, then stooped to pick it up and render it inert.

Kaslo threw back his cowl and removed his mask, opening the front of his suit to let out some of the trapped body heat that always built up when he wore one of the camouflage garments. Ferranian looked up at him, eyes and mouth making a triangle of circles, and said, "I know you!"

"You should," the op said. "I interviewed you once when I was investigating a smuggling ring that included some of your supercargoes." He gestured to the man on the floor. "He was the ringleader."

The magnate waved the memory away. "I'll hire you again, right now," he said, clutching the bicolour spiral to his chest. "Just get rid of him and say nothing about it. You can name your fee."

On the floor, the unconscious man took a sudden deep breath and began to stir. Kaslo knelt and stripped off Boronet's elision suit, then drew a holdtight from his belt and clipped together the groggy man's elbows and wrists. Kaslo's eyes were now level with Ferranian's, and he held the man's gaze.

"That's not how this works out," he said.

"Integrator!" Ferranian said. "Revive and—"

The device interrupted him. "A volante full of Provost's Department officers has just touched down outside. It has instructed me to disarm all defences. I have done so."

Heavy footsteps sounded from outside the room, and the gilded doors flew open. Sub-Inspector Fourna Houdibras stood in the doorway, fists on hips. "Well, well, well," she said. "What have we here?"

Come in, come in, said Lord Algrove. He stood at the door of the house he was renting in the exclusive Belletat district in the hills overlooking Indoberia. He barely glanced at the visitor's face before his gaze went to the wrapped package the man carried tucked against the hip of his spacer's overalls.

"Captain Boronet! How good to see you again," the aristocrat said as he closed the door. "I trust everything went as planned?"

"You provided the finest equipment," Boronet said, "and I, the qualities that a man needs to get things done."

"Excellent!" said Algrove, his eyes constantly flicking toward the package. "Come into the drawing room, and we will settle up."

He opened a door to a room furnished for hosting guests in comfort, and bowed Boronet in with a flourish of the hand that must have been fashionable on the odd little world he came from. After he had closed them both in, he indicated an array of flasks and decanters on a sideboard and asked the captain if he would take a drink. "I have some fine Falum wine, or a tot of Red Abandon, the spacer's drink, if you would prefer."

"I would prefer to do our business and depart," said the captain. He looked around the room and said, "Are we alone?"

"I have sent my servants away on errands and disengaged the house's integrator."

"Good," said Boronet. He placed the package on a small table and stood back. "There it is."

Algrove went eagerly to it, but before he unpeeled the wrapping, he turned and said, "And there will be no ... repercussions?"

"Not from Irczy Ferranian," said the spacer. "Let us say he is in no position to complain."

Still Algrove hesitated. "Not even if he is seized by pangs of conscience?"

"He is beyond all pangs."

"Excellent! Outstanding!" said the aristocrat, his fingers clawing away the heavy paper to reveal an octagonal case fashioned from precious metal and panes of crystal. Standing in it, on a plush armature, rested the bicolour spiral.

Lord Algrove's eyes enlarged. He lifted the case and regarded the treasure from several angles. When he spoke, it was in a whisper addressed only to himself. "At last!"

Captain Boronet made a sound to attract attention. "My fee," he said. "The documents conferring on me ownership of three Peregrinator-class freighters and a shipyard on Odlum's world."

"Of course," said Algrove. He carefully set down the case, went to an antique bureau, and opened a drawer. When he turned back to the spacer, his hand held a disorganizer. Without a further word, he pointed it at Boronet and pressed the activation stud.

Nothing happened. The Old Earther checked the weapon's settings then aimed and pressed again. But the disorganizer failed to convert the spacer into a glittering cascade of elemental particles.

A third voice spoke in the room. "It's been disarmed by the Provost's Department cruiser hovering over the house," said Erm Kaslo, standing in the doorway. He stepped into the room with Houdibras following. "These, however," he said, as he and the provost displayed heavy-duty shockers, "are highly functional."

Lord Algrove set down the disorganizer and drew himself up to full height. "I am a hereditary margrave of the first tier," he said. "I won't go into all of my titles and distinctions, but I can tell you that I am a second cousin to Dezendah Vesh, Archon Emeritus of Old Earth."

Houdibras smiled. "We'll be sure to let him know where to write you."

Purindath sat in the same chair she had first occupied in Erm Kaslo's workroom. She was relaxed, and her hat lay unmolested in her lap.

"Your sojourn on Fancheree seems to have agreed with you," Kaslo said.

"The mores are more strict than Novo Bantry's, but the climate was agreeable."

"I have transmitted a written report to the integrator at your late uncle's house, but I can give you the gist now, if you'd like."

"Please," said Kundlemaz.

"Once your … demise —"

"Execution, really," the young woman interrupted.

"Indeed," said Kaslo. "Once it was reported, the Commune stepped in and began an orderly disposition of your uncle's assets. The Erythreotic pearls collection went first, of course."

"But everything else remains unsold?" Kundlemaz said.

"Exactly. You had expressed no interest in keeping the collection."

"It brought my uncle's death. It might someday bring mine."

Kaslo continued his report. It had been assumed that the elder Kundlemaz had been murdered to bring his collection to auction. The bidders for the rarest of the rarities, the bicolour spiral, were soon identified as the most likely suspects. Because a spacer had delivered the message that drew the victim to the scene of the crime and because a freighter had been involved, suspicion fell most heavily on Irczy Ferranian. But Lord Algrove had offered an entire small planet for the prized pearl, and inquiries into the odd little world he hailed from revealed that its inbred aristocracy could be notoriously high-handed.

"Ferranian had contacts among the criminal underclass that has a parasitic relationship to interworld shipping," said Kaslo. "I discovered as much when I investigated a ring of corrupt supercargoes that was smuggling various substances and commodities from worlds where they were licit to worlds where they were forbidden.

"But Ferranian was smart. He put layers of intermediaries — cut-outs — between himself and the crimes. None of the ones we caught could be induced to testify against him, doubtless because he both paid and threatened them to keep quiet."

So the shipping magnate knew a corrupt spacer, Boronet — alias Gruen Podesko — who would do the murder for a fee. What he did not know was that Lord Algrove's lust for the bicolour spiral had led him to keep a close eye on Ferranian. The Old Earther had placed spies among Ferranian's employees and household servants. As soon as Ferranian had made his deal with Boronet, offering him a ship of his own as well as an upfront cash payment, Algrove's goons stepped out of the shadows.

"They used the same combination of threats and bribery. Algrove had recordings of Boronet and Ferranian conspiring to commit murder. That was the threat. The bribe was that he would give Boronet three ships — each better than the one Ferranian was offering — plus a shipyard. That would put Boronet on the first rung of the ladder to owning a fleet of freighters.

"All he had to do," Kaslo concluded, "was carry out Ferranian's plan to provoke the auction, then return a few days later to take the bicolour spiral off his first employer and hand it to his second."

"How did you know all this?" Kundlemaz said.

"Simple, plodding investigation, I must admit. Ships have to be registered somewhere and to someone. The freighter with the false name *Shangalang* turned out to be a ship named *Pride of New Adelaide*, owned by a company based on one of the moons of Holycow. That company was partly owned by a consortium, one of whose partners was involved in another partnership that did business exclusively with a firm in which Ferranian was a sleeping partner.

"A lot of this information was already on file from the smuggling case. Boronet's name soon came up, and we focused on him. While watching Boronet, we came across Lord Algrove's agents, traced them back to him, then scooped them up and pressured them for the facts."Kaslo rubbed his chin and gave a small chuckle. "It's remarkable what people will do to avoid a trial on Fancheree and the experience of Liberative Piacularity."

Kundlemaz grimaced. "I saw a couple of such 'experiences' while I was there," she said. "It was astonishing how long the malefactors lasted before the final unction."

Kaslo nodded. "Irczy Ferranian is cooperating fully with the provosts here on Novo Bantry so as not to face extradition. So is Boronet. They prefer lifelong detention in the Commune's contemplarium to Liberative Piacularity."

"And Lord Highsnoot?"

"Old Earth must be an interesting place. He is clearly accustomed to deference," said Kaslo, "and believes he will simply walk away. But the extradition documents from Fancheree have already arrived, and the Commune will not oppose. Your uncle was well regarded by many persons of influence."

Kundlemaz rose and made the gesture appropriate in Indoberia to the conclusion of their business. "I will instruct my integrator to disburse your fee as soon as the Commune returns my uncle's assets."

"Thank you," said the op. "And what about the bicolour spiral?"

Kundlemaz put on her cap and tugged it down at the front. "I haven't decided. What do you suggest?"

"Put it in a museum," Kaslo said. "Or smash it to powder."

The young woman quirked her mouth in thought and said, "I could give it to the Wardens Force on Fancheree. They are stern but highly creative."

Kaslo remembered the conversation with Frobe Mundun on the leased yacht. "They are, indeed."

"Perhaps they could devise some role for it to play in Lord Algrove's 'liberation'."

The op said, "I wouldn't be at all surprised."

Kundlemaz was heading for the door. Over her shoulder, she said, "But I imagine Algrove will be."

FEATURE INTERVIEW

Matthew Hughes

Pulp Literature: In your keynote speech for the 2001 Surrey International Writers' Conference, you described the tenacity and persistence that have allowed you to consistently make your living as a working writer. What does your 'no surrender' philosophy currently look like in your writing career?

Matthew Hughes: Same as ever. I'm still plugging away, still writing and selling. I have more readers now, more of a profile. It's possible that, after twenty-some years at this odd business, I will become an overnight success.

PL: On your blog, you quote the writer Louis L'Amour's advice: "Have your hero in trouble on page one." What are your preferred methods of cooking up trouble for your protagonist?

MH: My fiction is primarily character-based, although I use (and sometimes I abuse) well-established tropes of science fiction and fantasy. So my protagonists' troubles usually come at the hands of other characters. My protags are also often lower down the social scale than their adversaries — they're thieves, henchmen, hirelings, orphans — so there can be a social dynamic at play, too.

PL: *You also offer Elmore Leonard's writing advice, and I particularly appreciate the following: "Leave out all the passages that readers love to skip. (Those would be the ones you worked hardest on.)" What is the most painful literary excision you have had to make?*

MH: I can't think of one. I probably never have to kill my darlings, because they're never conceived in the first place. My first drafts are usually ninety percent per cent of the final product, and the revisions are more usually additions to the narrative than subtractions.

PL: *As a political and corporate speechwriter, you have put words in the mouths of politicians and titans of business. How does this compare to creating dialogue for characters of your own creation?*

MH: Very closely. I had no training as a speechwriter, but I was good at it from the first text I ever wrote — seconding debate on the Speech from the Throne that opened the 1974 Parliament. One draft and done. I had the useful knack of being able to hear a client's voice in my head as I wrote, and was also usually able to write from within that person's world view. I 'became' the client as I was writing for him or her. I do the exact same thing with fictional characters.

PL: *Do you story map or free-range write?*

MH: I am incapable of outlining. I start with a character in the character's normal situation, then I hand them a problem and see how they deal with it. One thing always leads to another, and eventually a story takes shape.

PL: *World building is integral to science fiction and fantasy writing, and it involves much more than setting alone. How do you approach being creatively expansive within the constraints of short fiction?*

MH: I only tell the reader what he or she needs to know to make the story work. I rarely info-dump. Instead, I show the made-up universe by detailing my characters' interactions with it.

PL: *In Issue 13, you describe yourself as "fundamentally a crime writer," and in 'The Bicolour Spiral' we see a blending of science fiction and crime writing. How do you create such literary alchemy?*

MH: Erm Kaslo is essentially Sam Spade in a space-opera universe. I get Humphrey Bogart's voice in my head as narrator and let the story unfold, based on what I know of criminality.

PL: *In your recently released novel,* What the Wind Brings, *you work another kind of alchemy, this time blending history with a touch of fantasy. Could you tell us how this story came to be?*

MH: Back in 1971, I came across a footnote in a university text about cross-cultural pollination. It was about how, contrary to the usual experience of castaways encountering a settled population, some African slaves shipwrecked on the jungle coast of Ecuador in the mid-1500s succeeded in forming a mixed society with the local indigenous peoples.

Three years before that, as a volunteer with the Company of Young Canadians, I had been a kind of castaway, pitching up in a northern Alberta Métis colony and living with two families there in nineteenth-century conditions—oil lamps, wood stove, water hauled from a lake—for several months. So the idea resonated.

The footnote made me think, "That could make a great historical novel." I'd had ambitions in that direction in my teens, and I kept the idea alive and embroidered on it from time to time over the next forty-odd years, while research on the events became more available in English-language scholarship.

In the meantime, my métier of writing about oddballs and outliers developed along with my literary skills. Eventually, I asked the Canada Council for $25,000, and when they gave me the grant, I wrote the book and polished it until I was satisfied it was the best work I've ever done.

ABSENT ARE THE CONSTELLATIONS MY FATHER PLUCKED FROM THE SKY

Sarah Summerson

Sarah Summerson *is a poet hailing from small-town central Pennsylvania. Her work has been featured in a variety of publications including* Confluence Magazine, OTHER Magazine, Tilde, Weaving the Terrain, *and peculiar. You can follow her on twitter @SarahSummersun for all the tidbits that couldn't find a home in a poem.*

$\mathcal{A}$BSENT ARE THE CONSTELLATIONS

MY FATHER PLUCKED FROM THE SKY

he drinks away the days
that make him older — the sun
grows longer — I am a pool of water
to ripple his own reflection
he walks the halls of my childhood home
his body echoes through my own
the hard thump of his bad leg
on the floors like a waltz
like he is not the angry drunk who
called
                    me
        up
                        and
                                        down
            the
                                pine
                soft
                                        stairs

obedience is a song
like the nightly rattle
of engine lights
on back roads

THE EXTRA: FRANKIE RAY AT THE GATES OF MONUMENT STUDIOS

Mel Anastasiou

Mel Anastasiou *writes mysteries, including the Fairmount Manor Mysteries and the Hertfordshire Pub Mysteries available at pulpliterature.com. For her novel* Stella Ryman *and the* Fairmount Manor Mysteries, *Mel won a Literary Titan Gold Book Award and was longlisted for the Leacock Memorial Medal for Humour. In Part 4 of the Monument Studios Mystery* The Extra, *Vancouver schoolteacher and hopeful actress Frankie Ray and her friend Connie Mooney find new dangers and mystery at Paradise Villas, a community of extras led by the powerful Loretta Desirée, veteran of King Samson's epic movies and queen of the extras.*

The Extra: A Monument Studios Mystery

Chapter One

April 1934
Paradise Garden Villas, Sunset Boulevard
Hollywood

Frankie Ray and Connie Mooney stepped into the crowded courtyard area at the centre of the Paradise Gardens bungalows. Frankie had never seen anything as lovely as the scene before her: warm air, a soft starry sky, and young men and women dancing and laughing in the tiled courtyard amid cottages and palms. Somebody had set up a gramophone, and conga music sounded two large drumbeats, like soft fists against her chest.

In the middle of the courtyard, a small fountain bloomed, with coloured lights reflected in its spray. A couple of dozen young people snaked in a line around the fountain, dancing the conga. *One-and-two-and-three. Kick!*

She felt Connie grip her arm and hold it for a few syncopated bars, and then some fellow reached out of the cluster of dancers and dragged Connie away. Frankie was left alone on the sidelines. She moved a little to the music, wanting more than anything in the world at that moment to be dancing too but feeling just as certain that she would never really fit in here—not like Connie, who had already vanished from view on the far side of the fountain.

And then, without quite understanding how, Frankie found herself in the arms of a man she'd never seen before. She was smoothly integrated into the snaking line of dancers. *One-and-two-and-three. Kick!*

She lost sight of the first man almost immediately, but it didn't seem to matter as she danced across the courtyard and around the fountain, her arms on somebody's shoulders and another pair of hands clasped around her waist. She looked over her shoulder, but all she could see of Connie—if it was Connie at all—was a flash of copper hair.

And now they were all circling the fountain in the centre of the courtyard, where music drowned out the splash of water. She looked about for the gramophone and spotted it on a table beside an old lady dressed in black and seated in a wicker chair. The old lady's hands lay clasped across the bosom of her black dress, and her eyes were shut. Electrical cords snaked from the phonograph around a stack of records at her feet.

Around the fountain—*one-and-two-and-three. Kick!*—the drumbeats pushed at Frankie, and she pushed back. The line ducked under a swinging row of Chinese lanterns.

A young man's voice shouted in her ear from behind. "Tell me, sister, what brings you to Paradise Gardens?

"We want to live here. We're actresses," she shouted back.

He laughed and called out, "The new girls are actresses."

The line returned a ragged shout, and Tom called, "Who ain't, darling?"

They conga-ed around the old woman's chair. Somebody turned up the sound. Clarinets blared, and Frankie could almost see the music, as if it were written by hand across the roofs of the little villas, the notes shining as they rose to join the stars in the deepening sky.

She stumbled on a loose brick and hung on tighter to the shoulders of the fellow in front of her.

Tom danced across the line, took her hands, and put them around his slender middle. He broke her free from the fellow behind her then spiralled her in and out, around and through the conga line, so that she hunched as she danced under the hands that made the chain. Once — twice! — a kick landed on her rear end, so she learned very quickly how to duck and dodge among the dancers. The sky spun overhead, and the bricks tripped her from underneath. Never in her life had Frankie been quite so happy or so homesick. This place, with its laughter and unreasoning welcome, with its heaving dancers under starry skies, with its flowers and firecrackers and Chinese lanterns, made her feel sorry for her old home the way she'd feel sorry for a poor cousin wearing brown at a wedding.

The music switched to a jazz ballad, and the line broke up into smaller, chattering groups.

"There she is." Tom cocked his head at the old woman next to the gramophone. "The landlady. I told her you helped me get a great quote from Gilbert Howard."

Meeting the landlady of Paradise Gardens seemed to Frankie to be another of those moments in life that resembled dancing the Carioca: you didn't want to get off on the wrong foot. Nevertheless, she tripped over the snarled extension cords and knocked the stack of records sideways so that they splayed across the old woman's feet. Frankie bent and shoved them back under the gramophone, conscious of the landlady's stare.

Frankie straightened up and introduced herself. "Ma'am, I'm sorry to begin so badly, but my friend Connie and I would like to move into Villa 7B if that's all right with you. We already have the key, and the previous occupant's permission. But I understand you're the one who makes the final decisions."

"Is that so?" The old woman bent, picked up a record, and set it on the gramophone. Bing Crosby crooned out 'June in January'.

"Yes, ma'am," Frankie answered smartly. "I used to be a substitute teacher, but now I hope to act in the movies. How much is the rent, please?"

"How long is a piece of string?" The old woman looked up at Frankie from under a black fringe of hair. Her mouth was too small for the current fashion, and her chin appeared to have been drawn by an uneven hand, but her eyes were pools of beauty, dark and heavily lined with kohl. "Don't talk business to the Queen, girl. Make a wish."

The landlady called herself a queen? Something deep inside Frankie whispered, *Oh dear.*

"May I ask, queen of what? I can't tell from your accent ..."

"The Voodoo Queen, the Robber Queen." The old woman had a pleasant voice, firm of timbre and clear of consonant. "You haven't told me your wish."

"I ..." Frankie frowned. She'd hoped to have a fair and honest conversation with the landlady about moving into Villa 7B. And now a wish? When she and Connie had been little, they had scorned anybody who found a magic ring or a fairy but couldn't think what they wanted. They'd always had three wishes picked out just in case. She couldn't remember what her first two had been, but the third was *a bottomless pocket of candy.*

"I wish to move into Paradise Gardens," Frankie said. "And I wish you'd tell me what I have to do to get in here. Tom said something about writing reports on the movements of movie stars …"

"Got any secrets?" the Queen asked.

Frankie answered that one with confidence. "In the last thirty-six hours, I've met two movie stars, both of them armed with a gun. I've seen an actor shoot a cameraman. Also, driving south to Hollywood, I picked up a studio head, barefoot on the side of the road, and sat in his gunshot son's lap for the better part of the day. I saw a married man kiss his movie-star fiancée and saw that same movie star hold him up at gunpoint for a chance to be the first woman director in Hollywood."

Once Frankie had finished, she felt a little grimy of character. She had revealed other people's secrets. She wished Connie were beside her, but she was over on the far side of the courtyard, making friends with everybody in sight. As usual, not a man within range could stay away from her. Flames burst from the open top of an oil drum not far from her as Tom, lit up as if by the belly of Hell, leaped back from the fire he'd started. He held aloft an emptied gas can to general applause from the young people. Frankie longed to join the group.

The Queen murmured, "What a lot of good secrets you know. How soon can you get more?"

Frankie took a deep breath. "Might I just *pay* the rent, please, and not worry about all these secrets?"

The Queen frowned. "No."

Frankie felt a pinch above her right elbow and Connie stepped up beside her. "Frankie, do you know, one of those girls over there is actually a fellow?" She gleamed in the firelight. "He says he's disguised as a waitress to spy on Clark Gable at Camillo's Fine Bar and Grille. What fun!" She looked past Frankie to the Queen and grinned. "You did his makeup, ma'am. The Queen of the Extras! Tom says your screen name is Loretta Desirée. Gosh, what a moniker."

"I give wishes, you know." Loretta Desirée, Queen of the Extras, inclined her head. "What do you wish for, pretty red-haired girl? Riches, fame, or love?"

"Fame?" Connie frowned. "Do you think it's right to offer me wishes you can't grant?"

With a warning look, Frankie kicked Connie in the ankle. Connie kicked back.

The old woman held out both hands to them. "Me? What has it to do with me? This is how it is—you say a wish, and it comes true."

Connie said, "Okay, I'm hungry. I wish for something to eat."

Over by the oil drum, Tom put two fingers in his mouth and whistled. Connie turned in time to catch something small he threw to her. She looked at the bit of sausage and popped it in her mouth.

"Just what I asked for. You grant a good wish, my queen. Go on, Frankie, wish."

"I already did. My wish is to live here." Frankie shook her head. "She didn't grant that one, though."

Connie turned on the Queen. "Then you get another one. Doesn't she?"

The Queen said, "One more wish."

Was it any more foolish to make a wish to the Voodoo Queen of the Extras than to wish on the evening star? Frankie breathed in the smell of spiced meat. She screwed her eyes shut. What should she wish for—riches, fame, or love? She wanted all three. And a bottomless pocket of candy, too. But at that moment, as Crosby crooned and sausages popped and sizzled on the fire, what Frankie desired more than anything else was far more magical.

Frankie said, "I wish to act in the movies."

"Granted, provisionally." The Queen of the Extras tapped her nose. "You do know what happens with wishes. You lose your soul."

Frankie laughed out loud. "My dad's in charge of mine, and you couldn't pry anything away from him with a crowbar."

The fire in the oil drum crackled. The Queen stood up and yawned. Twenty years dropped away from her. "Not bad. Not bad at all for a first day. You and your pretty friend will fit right in with my lovely band of young monkeys. You have the key to Villa 7B? Use it."

"Thank you," Frankie said.

"You're welcome. And since you've got it, and nobody else here has a dime, it will cost you a hundred dollars for three months' rent, in advance."

It was far more than she'd anticipated. It was, in fact, the sort of rent you might expect to pay at a high-end hotel back home. Even in Hollywood, there had to be cheaper accommodation. Was it worth the investment? Frankie knew what Champ would say: *Frankie, keep your dollars close to your chest and deal yourself out of any bet that might lose them.* There wasn't much Champ didn't know about money.

But she'd made this money herself by substitute teaching. She fiddled a hundred dollars out of the wad in her pocket, leaving four tens behind, and handed the money to the Queen.

The Queen slid the bills up one voluminous sleeve. "You'll be glad when I remember these hundred dollars, down the road when *you* don't have a dime for the rent. In the meantime, learn how to keep an eye open for gossip. As for the movies, you start tomorrow."

"Sure thing." The woman was making fun of Frankie's dreams and ambitions. But she found she didn't much care — she had Villa 7B and all her future ahead of her. Or maybe she was just too overwhelmed to mind. Anyway, queens did as they wished.

The record came to its scratchy end, the needle bumping against the centre of the disc. And in the sudden silence, a cracking sound rang out, like somebody had shot off a gun.

A gunshot. Somewhere near Paradise Gardens. Frankie almost laughed — everything about Hollywood was so far over the top. Even night noises sounded like something in the movies. Back home, she'd have known it was a car backfiring or a door slamming shut. Here in Hollywood, she'd have sworn it was a gunshot.

She laughed at herself as Tom dashed over, bearing oily newspaper spread with bits of sausage.

"We made it. We're here. We're in Villa 7B," Frankie told him. He slapped her shoulder and kissed the top of the Queen's head. Frankie bent and picked up a record that had slipped out of the fallen stack. She read the title and asked Tom, "Do you dance the Carioca?"

"Never on a first date, darling. Put on 'Moonglow'. Tom flipped through the stack of records. Frankie removed 'The Heebie-Jeebie Blues' and handed Tom 'The Carioca'.

"Go to bed," the Queen advised her. "If you want to be in the movies tomorrow, go to bed."

"I don't want to go to bed. Not ever again," Frankie told her. "Even though you're probably right. But it's my first night in Hollywood, and I don't want to miss anything."

The Queen nodded. "Most young people don't take advice. I certainly didn't. Listen. Here's some more. Don't fall in love in Paradise Gardens."

"All right." Frankie swayed, eyes closed, as the first notes of the Carioca rang out. *Don't fall in love in Paradise Gardens* was one bit of advice that the diamond ring in her pocket guaranteed she'd follow.

At a touch to her sleeve, she turned to face a young man she'd not seen before. "I don't know you," she said. "But I'm Frankie Ray."

"I know who you are," he said. "Frankie Ray, do you dance the Carioca?"

"I do."

He was about her height, so she looked him straight in the eye. The fact that he was fair in his colouring from top to toe — suit, face, and hair — made his person a neutral palette for the coloured lights to play upon.

"But I should say that I've only practised the Carioca with other girls," she told him. "And usually I lead."

"Do what you need to do," he said.

As the strings rose, the grey man took her in his arms, and she danced the Carioca around the fountain, sometimes leading, sometimes following, her coat billowing out around her as if it were made of feathers. Finally, as he dipped her and swung her back onto her feet, she got around to asking his name.

The grey man hesitated, probably due to the switch in lead. "Eugene Ellery, that's what they call me."

Eugene Ellery! It sounded as phony as *Billie Starr.* Frankie slid backwards and missed the fire by an inch. She joked, "Does everybody choose their own name in Hollywood?"

"Doesn't it sound like a natural name?" He smiled into her eyes. "Doesn't it sound like a name a couple would give to their little boy?"

"Nothing unnatural in alliteration," she said. "You know, they say a man will tell you everything you need to know about him the first time you meet."

"I'm a faithful fellow," Eugene told her.

"An attractive quality. I'm an engaged woman, myself."

She'd bet her bottom dollar he was a writer — a screenwriter. She took three quick steps backwards and dipped him, just for a change. He smelled of Burma-Shave, like Champ. "I want to be an actress."

"I see. Quite a lot of nonsense, the movies, don't you find?"

She didn't mind a difference of opinion while dancing the Carioca. "Then you're not a writer? Or an actor?"

"Aren't we all acting, all the time?" He laughed and dipped her in turn. "Great Harry, that sounded condescending. Let's change the subject."

Eugene Ellery's timing was perfect, because the music soared just then into a bit that Frankie had practised to perfection, and so she took the lead back and spun them round the fountain. When the Carioca stopped at last, Eugene squeezed Frankie's arm and melted into the group around the fire.

"Has he gone home?" She took a swig from the flask Tom proffered.

"Who? Our Eugene?" Tom looked at her sideways.

Frankie nodded. There was still a group gathered round the fire, but their numbers were dwindling. The Queen was nowhere to be seen. A couple of girls closed up the gramophone and packed records into a small leather trunk with handles. On the far side of the fire, a few of the fellows had produced musical instruments: a banjo and a couple of harmonicas.

Tom said, "Eugene Ellery lives in Villa 7A right there, doll. He's the boy next door to you two. Look, there's your 7B."

Frankie looked. Villa 7B was the bungalow on the far side of the patio, the one closest to the Garden of Allah on the next lot, not far from the bushes in which she'd so recently hidden to watch Gilbert Howard recite Webster's beautiful, chilling words. Villa 7B was hers. Hers and Connie's. The windows were all dark, of course, and because it was a place she'd taken without looking first, the unlit cottage should have had an empty look. Its windows should have looked like eyes, blank and strange and a little scary. Instead, 7B looked like a sweet loyal dog lying in the shadows at the edge of the brick patio, waiting for her to come home.

Frankie took a deep breath of smoky night air and released it. Then, feeling herself fading as surely as the final titles of a movie, she stumbled in the darkness along the walk to the Model A. Connie found her before she'd hauled the suitcases halfway back along the path. Frankie gladly handed over half the load. Between them, suitcases in hand, they managed the door to their bungalow.

She paused in the doorway of Villa 7B, taking in, with enormous pleasure, the sight of the green plaid sofa framed by matching plaid curtains. To her right, there was a dainty kitchenette, with a kettle on the stovetop and a toaster trailing its cord down to the linoleum floor. Beside that was the tiny bathroom, then the door to the bedroom and a back door next to the sofa. With a whoop of delight, Frankie dropped her case in the middle of the floor and toppled onto the sofa. Outside, the harmonicas hummed a sorrowful tune, but nothing could make Frankie feel blue at that moment.

Already she felt quite the mistress of the house. She stuck out her legs and slouched low, with her head on the back of the sofa and her hands in her pockets, where her fingers played for a moment with her forty dollars. She was tired, but she wasn't foolish, so she tucked her money safely under the sofa cushions. The gun was safe where it was, in the bushes behind their villa.

Connie swung open one of two doors to the right of the sitting room by the kitchenette. "The bedroom's cute, and there are twin beds and bedding. The bathroom's cuter. Don't know if it's clean."

"It's perfect. It's ours. And there's a toaster." Frankie kicked off her shoes and pulled her feet up beside her on the sofa, resting her head on the arm. It smelled a little of somebody else's hair. She would go to bed soon, but just now she was keen to sit and listen to a few of the fellows crooning melodies outside in the square. She drifted and was only just aware of a blanket sliding over her as Connie lifted Frankie's feet and tucked them inside.

Connie whispered, "Are we in Hollywood or in Heaven?"

"Both," Frankie murmured. "We're sailing a sea of stars."

Moonlight through the living room window woke her. It must have been very late, because the music had stopped and the moon had moved across the sky. She found her way to the little bathroom and used it. She washed her hands and face in the dark. She considered joining Connie in the room they were to share but decided she was enjoying her sleepy solitude too much. The darkness and silence felt as cosy as the blanket around her, and she sat up for a moment or two, her chin and arms on the back of the sofa, admiring the gleam of the oranges on the little tree in the backyard they shared with Villa 7A.

It was the tree they shared with Eugene Ellery. Frankie yawned. Eugene Ellery, she repeated to herself. And, as if by magic — again by magic! — there he was. Eugene Ellery was standing in their shared yard in the middle of the night like the answer to a Vancouver maiden's prayer — if such a maiden were not engaged to somebody else. His back was turned to 7B, and surely he didn't know she was watching him standing below 7A's rear window with a shepherd's crook in his hand.

Yes, with crook held upright, he might have been keeping watch over his flock, although there was nothing in front of him but the short expanse of their shared lawn and the hedge that separated Paradise Gardens from the Garden of Allah.

But it couldn't have been a shepherd's crook. That was silly. That was the sort of thing that came into your head when you were half-asleep in a new place. Eugene Ellery was holding a tall stick upright in his right hand, that was all. It was probably a walking stick. Or a shovel. She blinked heavy lids. Of course, he was holding a shovel.

The weight of her head dragged her back into sleep, and she dreamed of riches and fame, love and candy.

Chapter Two

Frankie woke up in a little bedroom so thick with green light filtered through the curtains that she might have been in a deep forest. It was impossible to say what time she'd abandoned the sofa and crawled into her own bed here in Villa 7B, nor could she guess the hour now. At some point during the night she must have thrown off her skirt and blouse to sleep in her petticoat, because there they were, tangled in her blanket. She turned over and bunched up the pillow under her cheek. Here she was — in Hollywood. Settled in Paradise Gardens!

Never was there a girl as lucky as she. Everyone should be so lucky … Why not? She understood, of course, that the world was in a tough situation. She hadn't forgotten the lines of cars hung about with earthly goods and thin-faced children, nor the open doors near the waterfront back home that served soup and bread to men lined up, holding their hats against their chests.

But if money was scarce, good fortune was free. *There's plenty of luck to go around*, she wanted to tell those thin-faced kids hanging on the running boards of the Okie's cars. *Leave home and pursue it. Break the rules like a piñata, and the luck will come a-tumbling down.* You didn't need money, though she was glad of her forty dollars under the sofa cushions in the living room. It wasn't money that had gotten her this far. It was persistence.

A bird called outside the open window. She sat up in bed and remembered how, when she was little, her father used to wake her with the old rhyme about the birdie with a yellow bill, the one that ended, *Ain't you 'shamed, you sleepyhead?* As she blinked sleep away, the green plaid curtains lifted just enough to let in the morning light, then fell back again. Connie's bed, the second one, was empty, and Frankie got the sense that she might be missing out on things on her first morning in Hollywood. The door to the bedroom stood ajar, and she smelled that Connie was burning toast for breakfast …

An unwelcome thought interrupted these observations: *I'm not supposed to be here.*

Sure I am, she countered silently. She stretched both arms and legs out wide, feeling larger than life in the little green bedroom. She gathered the bedclothes into her arms, chenille coverlet and all, ready to make her bed. Instead, a bubble of happiness growing inside her, she lumped them onto the floor and left the bed unmade.

Snatching up her coat from where it lay crumpled at one end of the sofa, she buttoned it over her petticoat. She called out as she left the bedroom, "Hey, Connie, what does it mean if you dream about a handsome man holding a shovel?"

"It means you ate burnt sausages before bedtime. Hey, Frankie"—and here Connie put on her radio announcer's voice—"*how do you know you've got a really great cup of coffee?*"

Frankie intoned, "*It's good to the la-a-ast drop.*"

A short stack of burnt toast at her elbow, Connie leaned over the little table by the front window and set two places with bright blue dishes. In the middle of the table, a bowl full of oranges glowed like a good idea. The little kettle bubbled on the stovetop.

I should be back home in Vancouver. The unwelcome thought elbowed back in. *I should be sitting in a ladylike way on the porch step beside my red geranium. I should be waiting for Champ to come around.*

No, darn it, I should not.

Frankie shut the bathroom door on the smell of singed crusts and strong tea. She gave herself a quick wash in the little pink tub—hardly more than a sponge bath, but, after almost four days on the road, Wordsworth had it right: *Oh, the difference to me!*

On a hook by the little window, somebody had left a threadbare towel embroidered with a red strawberry and two green leaves. She dried what she could of herself with it and put her coat back on. Then she took a good look at her face in the mirror over the sink. Seashells glued around its circumference made her reflection look like a mermaid peering out to see how the folks in Hollywood lived. Hollywood folks: that's what Frankie and Connie had turned into overnight. Now *there* was magic for you.

Still wearing her coat, Frankie pulled two of the three copper-wire chairs up to the table. She took a big bite of dry burnt toast. It stuck to the inside of her teeth and had to be washed down with black tea. Connie made the worst toast of anybody she knew. Her method was to hold one finger on each knob of the flop-down toaster until the first lick of smoke signalled it was ready. Even so, for atmosphere, Frankie decided it was about the best breakfast she'd ever eaten.

It's about eight o'clock in the morning. I should be running out to the vegetable truck to buy parsnips and potatoes to peel for my father's supper. But she was here in Hollywood, and that was that.

Connie poured herself and Frankie a second cup of tea. "To us."

"Yes, ma'am." Frankie clinked a blue cup against Connie's. She was pleased to find the sturdy blue crockery in Villa 7B's little kitchen. A kitchen in a furnished suite ought to come fully equipped. Connie's mom had packed them a paper sack of tea bags from Vancouver.

"Where did you get the bread?" Frankie asked.

For an answer, the door to Villa 7B snapped open, and Tom strolled inside.

"I've fixed those wires in your car so the key will work again. And this is for you, the new birds."

He set a little glass pot on the table before them, bent over between the two girls to lift the glass lid and, with a little tin spoon, scooped a bit of gem-red jam onto Connie's piece of toast. Frankie pulled her coat tighter around her and decided that privacy was a reasonable exchange for strawberry jam on your first morning in town.

Tom pulled the third chair up to the table. "Doris keeps us in jam. She works in the Beverly Hills Hotel on odd weekends, disguised as a bellboy with a waxed moustache, since she got herself fired from room service for eating a pound of steak tartare. She saw Clark Gable last week with a fish as long as your arm. The chef cooks the fish Gable catches, but the lady who dined with him wasn't his wife. No, sir."

"Gosh." Frankie passed Tom a cup of tea while Connie peered into the jam pot.

He went on, "Mickey in Villa 5B gets the day-old bread. He delivers for a bakery to all the biggest houses while we're still in dreamland. One time he saw Katherine Hepburn in men's pyjamas. She was all alone, though, so there was no story that he could sell."

"I think men's pyjamas would be comfy if they weren't too big for a girl," Frankie said. "Maybe I'll get me some."

"Me, too," Connie said. "When we're in the money. Yellow pyjamas with a green stripe. Say, where do these oranges come from?"

"From you," Tom said. "You've got the best tree in Paradise Gardens, right out back."

Tom took three oranges from the bowl and began to juggle them (the ceiling was a little low for the trick, Frankie thought), just before one careened off, bounced on the plaid sofa under the window, and rolled into a corner. He ran to retrieve them.

A girl with honey-coloured hair appeared in the window over the table and introduced herself as Doris. She leaned in and accepted a piece of toast.

"Hey, chums, pleased to meet you. Nine-o'clock call on the Monument lot, Tom." Doris talked around a mouthful of toast, her elbows resting on the windowsill. "Powder your nose and meet us on Sunset Boulevard in an hour. Where are you two girls from?"

"Vancouver, Canada. You?" Frankie spread jam on more toast and handed a piece to Doris and a second to Tom to take with him as he ducked out the door.

Doris took the toast with thanks. "Wichita, Kansas. I came west with a couple of friends."

Frankie started. *Three of them*, then. Marietta Valdes had said almost the same words on the cliff above the ocean, just before she'd driven off with Gilbert Howard in that long Cadillac. And Blanche Carver had said much the same about her own arrival in Hollywood, a number of years before Marietta's advent. Frankie murmured, "Everybody comes to Hollywood in threes."

Doris said, "Sure. *Or* in pairs, like you gals, *or* quadruples, *or* on their own. My two friends went back home to Wichita a week later, but here I am like a bump on a log. I'll never go home now."

"Me neither," Connie said. "How soon can we sign up to be extras?"

Tom popped back in, snatched another piece of toast and jam, and said, "Girls, you're in. You start as extras *today*, courtesy of the Queen."

"We're extras? In the movies?" Frankie sat back hard against the wire chair. They'd been in Hollywood less than twenty-four hours. Frankie thought, a little wildly, that she could have used a little time to get used to the idea. "The Queen granted my wish after all."

"We're in the movies today? Jiminy." Connie stood up, her hand at her throat.

"You girls are mighty lucky." With a smacking noise, Tom kissed the crown of Frankie's head. "We leave in half an hour."

"Half an hour." Doris swore. "I'd better rinse out my snood." She grinned and ducked away from the window.

Connie swept the dishes off the table and into the sink. "I love you, Tommy boy. Now beat it while Frankie puts some clothes on under that coat. We've got half an hour to get ready!"

"Got an iron?" Frankie crammed the last bit of toast down her throat. Tom galloped off for the iron.

Frankie was half-dressed by the time it warmed up. She located a wall-mounted, pull-down ironing board in the kitchenette and did a slapdash job on their two clean dresses, pounding out the worst of the wrinkles with the flat of the iron. The familiar housekeeping task calmed her down and sped up her movements. With fifteen minutes to spare while Connie made herself up, Frankie checked that her forty dollars were still snug and safe under the sofa cushions in the living room. Then she rushed off the back stoop onto the sunny lawn and flung her stockings back and forth to dry them. Under her bare feet the lawn felt coarse and already dry, though perhaps they didn't have dew in California. Or in Heaven, either. She gazed at the orange-laden branches of the small but enterprising tree in their little backyard.

Opportunities grow like oranges on a tree, she thought, *and all you have to do is pick them.* Still swinging her stockings, Frankie caught sight of a glitter of turquoise through the hedge that divided their yard from the Garden of Allah, its swimming pool, and the rich and famous who lived there. Maybe she'd live there too, someday, right next door to Gilbert Howard. Just now she was happy to stand exactly where she was in easygoing Paradise Gardens, drying her wet stockings. The sky was blue, and the leaves were green. The air shone as bright as the neon ceiling in the Dominion Theatre.

Then, for the first time that morning, Frankie remembered the gun she'd dropped in the bushes between The Garden of Allah and Paradise Gardens. There would be time to find it soon—all the time in the world. She might look for it that night, if they got back from the studio before sunset. And if not, there would be the next day to search for it, and the next … With nobody to hear her, her stockings waving madly round her head, she sang 'Dora Heart' out loud. *"Hi de Ho de Hee —"*

Behind her, somebody cleared his throat.

Frankie jumped. She turned around. There between their two villas stood the fellow next door, Eugene Ellery. His skin appeared paler in daylight than when they'd danced the night before. Today, with his slender shoulders under a well-cut jacket, he appeared almost delicate, and Frankie hoped that he wasn't ill. But although TB made you delicate, it also gave you a high colour, and Eugene certainly didn't have that. Frankie thought him very handsome, but nobody in the world was handsome enough to distract her from the happiness of the moment.

Still, he was very handsome.

Eugene cleared his throat while the cuffs of his grey summer-weight suit flapped in the morning breeze around his shiny brogues. "Could you spare a few minutes, Frankie?"

Frankie screwed up her eyes. "Sure thing, but it'll have to wait," she said.

He looked down at his well-polished shoes. "It won't take long."

In about twelve minutes, she would have to meet the rest of the extras on Sunset Boulevard. "I've got a nine o'clock call," she explained.

"There's something buried out back," he said.

She frowned. "In your garden?"

"Our shared garden, yes. And it can't wait for later." He met her eyes. "I need a witness while I find out what it is. I need your help, neighbour."

She was about to ask him to find somebody else in Paradise Gardens to help when she realized that he had called her *neighbour*. And now that she looked more closely at him, she saw the last thing she would have expected. In Eugene Ellery's eyes she saw not just his appeal, but the appeal of her neighbour Hazel back home as she begged for help finding a photograph of her dead brother, whose face she could no longer remember. He reminded her of the way Irene had looked when she came to Frankie, at the end of her rope with her wandering husband. And her neighbour Mattie, the bank teller, asking her why the hell he'd been fired, not knowing that the whole world believed his fingers danced in the till. Even on her first morning in Hollywood, with just a few moments before she had to leave, Frankie couldn't let a neighbour down. On Thirty-sixth Avenue or on Sunset Boulevard, to dishonour a neighbour's plea was unthinkable.

So, obligingly and with a certain curiosity—but keeping count of the time—Frankie slung her stockings over her shoulder. She followed Eugene across the grass to 7A, where he stopped. A little breeze ruffled the leaves of the orange tree behind 7B and lifted the white silk ascot Eugene wore at his neck. Looking down at the grass, he said, "There's something buried there."

Frankie took a step to one side. Sure enough, she made out the shape of a low mound where the grass had been cut away, perhaps with the edge of a shovel, and then relaid. The mound extended about six feet from the centre of the lawn toward the hedge that divided Paradise Gardens from the Garden of Allah. The buried shape was about a foot and a half wide, she guessed, and not quite straight.

She had to leave for the studio in ten minutes.

"It might be a dog," Frankie suggested.

He sent her an oblique glance.

She added, "It would of course need to be a very large dog."

"It might be a water tank," he said. "The kind they collect rainwater in, buried by former tenants."

"You're quite observant," Frankie said.

"A water tank of that sort is about the size of a human torso."

The sun was growing warmer by the minute, but Frankie suddenly felt cold.

"I'd better dig," Eugene said.

"With what?" Frankie followed his glance to the shovel leaning up against the side of Villa 7A. If the set-ups were the same in both cottages, the handle just touched his bedroom window. So, either she had dreamed a prophetic, Joseph-like dream or—

She heard Connie shout her name, and called back, "In a minute!" She turned to Eugene and looked him dead in the eye. "I'm just wondering why you were standing out here in the middle of the night, holding a shovel."

He inclined his head. "I suppose not mentioning that I'd done so was—"

"A lie. Of omission. Why?" Frankie watched him carefully, but Eugene's calm eyes and smooth brow gave no hint of his feelings.

"People lie from greed, revenge, or love," he said. "Or from fear. So I've always understood. But, in my case, I just didn't want to give you the wrong idea. Last night, I was going to dig up the mound, but on reflection I thought I ought to have—"

"A witness." She nodded her understanding.

Eugene crouched down by the middle of the mound in the grass. Barehanded, he tugged up a roundish divot of turf. It came up neatly and fell in a lump at his side.

From inside Villa 7B Connie called out, "Six minutes."

Frankie watched Eugene dig. It seemed that everything in the sunlit world of Paradise Gardens was still except the gentle, mouse-like sound of his fingers brushing at the dirt. He let out a long breath.

"I thought so," he said, hunkered over his bit of the mound.

"Is it a water tank?" But she knew it wouldn't be.

"No, it's not so much a water tank." Eugene brushed a little soil off of something flat and pale he'd uncovered.

Frankie looked hard at it, at the three little valleys next to a three inch-square plane planted with sparse, dark hair. Eugene Ellery dusted the thing he'd uncovered, but he couldn't remove the dirt from the creases in the knuckles.

Feeling ill, Frankie sat back on her heels. Eugene was touching the body. His hands lay across the corpse's fingers as if trying to warm them.

With heartache, she remembered the time she and Connie had found a robin under one of the great elms outside Frankie's house. She had never forgotten the soft prick of the ruffled pinfeathers as she picked it up. The two little girls knelt in the dirt, and first one, and then the other, attempted to stroke it back to life. In the end, they named the dead bird *Tige* and buried it with kindness, as Connie said, in a Buster Brown shoebox in

the dirt under the back steps of the Rays' house. Frankie had been hard-pressed to stop Connie from kicking the next cat she met. And to stop herself from doing so as well.

Eugene rose to his feet. He looked down at his palms and then shoved his hands deep into his pockets. "Let us not give in to emotion."

"I'll do what I want," Frankie answered. She closed her eyes. She hardly knew what she was saying. "My father says that if emotions made sense, we wouldn't need them. Logic would see us through every circumstance."

"*Four minutes!*" Connie's voice sounded more urgent than ever, but this time Frankie couldn't find the words to respond.

She felt a warm breath against her cheek. Frankie opened her eyes to see Eugene Ellery's face up very close to her own. His grey eyes showed pink at the inside corners.

"Go," he said. "Join the others at your nine-o'clock call. I'm sorry I've upset you. Still, you've been my witness. My insurance, now that I can call the local police. You may have to give them a statement."

"Yes. Although I hardly know what I'd say. Aren't you going to ...?" She gestured to the patch of uncovered flesh: the corpse's white hands with their dirty knuckles. "Aren't you going to uncover him?"

"Him?"

She nodded. "The hairs on a woman's fingers would be softer."

"Him, then." Eugene Ellery helped Frankie to her feet. "There's no sense in uncovering him. We'll let the local police handle it. Poor fellow."

"But if he's buried in your backyard ..." She couldn't finish without asking whether he was the one who had buried that body. But then, why dig a dead man up again? You'd have to be insane to do such a thing, and there was one thing she knew: Eugene Ellery was not crazy.

"Our shared backyard," he reminded her. He untied his white silk ascot from around his neck and wiped their hands clean, first hers and then his.

She asked, "Who do you think this was?"

He crushed the silk into his jacket pocket. "It's bound to be somebody's old aunt."

"Uncle," she corrected him.

"Somebody's old uncle, then, who died, and there was no money set aside for a funeral. It happens a lot in common spaces these days. Although usually they bury them deeper …"

"So he's buried in the yard like a dog?" Frankie said.

"People love their dogs," Eugene pointed out. "Look, I don't need to give you any more nightmares about shovels. We'll leave him covered. Go. Do what you were going to do."

"I don't know if I can." Frankie took a deep breath. "I don't know if I can drive at all right now. I'll wait with you for the police."

"Well, didn't they tell you? I am the police." Eugene Ellery made the sort of gesture that accompanied, in Frankie's experience, a person's reluctance to explain things she wanted to know. "I'm a policeman. Not from around here, though. This is not my jurisdiction. Still, now I've seen the body, I can call out the local coppers."

Connie called out through the back door, "Frankie, if you're not ready, the extras will leave without us!"

Was it wrong to leave the body here? To go off like a snap of busy fingers to be a Hollywood extra, caring about nothing but herself? Frankie would have liked to ask the dead man what he thought. She would say, *Excuse me, sir. This is an important day for me, but I guess I could say the same for you. Would you like me to stay? I'll give up my first day as an extra in the movies if you need me to.*

She tried to imagine how it would be to lie dead in the grass and dirt while a young woman, with all her life ahead of her, asked that question. She could not. All she knew was that she owed the dead man something.

Frankie put out her hand and touched the three pale fingers. They were cool, but not cold. They were much the same temperature as the cool morning air. Shivering, she forced herself to leave her fingers on his for another moment. "I'm sorry you had to die, sir," she said. "I don't know what to do right now to show my respect. Should I wait here with you and Eugene?"

It was hard to put oneself into a dead man's shoes. She closed her eyes and waited for an answer.

When a moment later the answer came, she didn't feel any sort of ghostly spookiness. Nor any sort of warning. The words simply came to her from inside herself: *You owe me nothing. One person waiting at my side is company enough on a sunny morning.*

Frankie stood up. She took a deep breath and turned to walk back to Villa 7B.

From behind her, Eugene Ellery said, "Frankie Ray, you are a very unusual young woman. You've earned my ..." She looked back at him as he finished. "My loyalty."

Conscious of the gravity of Ellery's stare, she turned her back on the shallow grave and stumbled up the back stoop of Villa 7B, where she found Connie in a frenzy of impatience lest they be left behind when the other extras left for the studios. Frankie snatched up her shoes and car key. *Hurry, Frankie, hurry.* She dug her lipstick out of her coat pocket, but her hands were too unsteady to apply it. She hung her coat on the hook inside the bathroom door—it fell to the floor, and she hooked it up again. At the last moment, she remembered her engagement ring. There was no time to hide it in the sofa with her forty dollars, so she slipped her ring into the pocket of her green-and-blue dress.

"Come on, pokey," Connie urged. "They're going to leave without us."

"Put my lipstick on for me, will you? My hands are shaking."

"We're just extras, you know. But I'm aflutter, too." Connie obliged and then peered at her handiwork. "My big chance might come any time. Blot your lipstick on your wrist."

With Connie at her side, Frankie hustled out through the villas toward Sunset Boulevard. She couldn't stop thinking about the pale, grubby hand she'd watched Eugene uncover. And she couldn't stop picturing Eugene as she'd seen him the night before, leaning on his shovel under a starry sky.

Eugene is a policeman. He wouldn't bury a body in his own backyard. She was right about that, anyway, and she was also certain that Eugene had been wrong about something besides the gender of the corpse. The person buried—presumably with kindness—in the backyard had not been old. Those were not the knobby knuckles of an old man.

She caught sight of Tom's blue sweater vanishing around the corner of Villa 12A, where the blonde woman who played jazz records and threw dishes lived. She and Connie caught up with him under the swinging sign for Paradise Gardens. Out on the road, a pickup truck loaded with young people huffed and sagged as Tom leapt in. "Follow us," he said.

"Why don't we go along in the truck?" Connie stood on the running board of the Model A. "It looks like fun."

"We have to meet the Queen to sign up at Central Casting." Frankie slumped behind the steering wheel and fumbled with the key. "I'm kind of tired. Would you mind driving?"

"Sure thing." Connie scrambled over her into the driver's seat. "Off we go." Connie squeezed Frankie's shoulder and started up the Model A. Frankie was grateful for its loyal ignition and companionable chuddering. Before the truck and the Model A had covered fifty yards, the crowd of young extras in the truck bed ahead of them had begun to sing: *"Come away with me, Lucille, in my merry Oldsmobile . . ."*

Connie sang along. Frankie sat and brooded.

"Down the road of life we'll fly . . ."

The body in the backyard was not an obstacle. It was a sad fact of life. In these hard times, a man had died. For lack of money to pay for a funeral, somebody had buried him in a beautiful spot beside an orange tree. Worse things than that could happen in these times of want and need. She remembered the Okies in their dusty rattletraps the day before, and the sharp bones and thin face of the smiling boy who'd waved at her.

"Automo-bubbling, you and I . . ."

She must pull herself together. She felt she owed it to Connie — and, strangely, to the dead man — to keep her chin up. She must not tremble. She would not cry. Neither action was professional, except under directorial guidance for the sake of a scene. If she was an actress as she claimed, she ought to be able to wear the face of a girl who hadn't seen a dead body.

"Come on, gloomy," Connie urged her. "Sing out so that the others can hear us. *You can go as far as you like with me, in my merry Oldsmobile!*"

Frankie watched out for a place for Connie to park. Once she entered the studios, she would have to act a part. She would have to look and behave like a girl who still believed, as she had that morning under the little orange tree behind Villa 7B, that everybody in the world could be lucky.

Chapter Three

The Monument Studios sound stages stood just off Sunset Boulevard, strong and windowless, looking to Frankie's eye like monolithic rectangles of white, store-bought cake. Beyond these she saw what looked like the roofs and gilded pinnacles of an ancient city movie set. Frankie walked between Connie and the Queen and tried her utmost to conjure up the awe and thrill she ought to feel on her first morning as an extra. She felt nothing but sorrow for the dead man in Villa 7A's backyard.

"You're awfully quiet." Connie touched Frankie's sleeve. "Say, what in the world is that?"

Above the wall that separated one set from another, the black ears and snout of a dog-faced Egyptian god pointed straight at them.

Frankie said, "It's a statue on a set, I guess."

Loretta Desirée, the Queen of the Extras, put an arm over each of the girls' shoulders. "It's *the* set — of King Samson's greatest film, *Ambition*. 1928. I was an extra the day they burned the virgins alive! Girls, I was the first to fling myself into the flaming abyss."

Connie said, "How exciting! Did you land on a mattress?"

"Two!" The Queen's eyes lit up, and then dimmed. "It breaks my heart to think that tonight's the night they're going to burn the set itself to film the big city fire scene in *The Emperor of New York*."

"Burning down the set! What a travesty!" Connie scowled. "They should keep those Egyptian statues forever. They ought to charge visitors money to get in and see them, like a museum."

At the thought of burning down *Ambition*'s beautiful set, Frankie tried to feel angry. She could not. All she could think of was that poor dead man in the back garden.

"Are you all right, Frankie?" The Queen frowned. "Your colour isn't good. And you look awfully sad."

"Frankie always comes through," Connie assured her.

"Sure." Frankie pulled herself together as best she could.

"First-day jitters! Without 'em, you'd hardly be human." The Queen gave their shoulders an encouraging squeeze and hurried them on toward the extras' marshalling area. Because they'd had to stop off at Central Casting, the three were already late. But both were just now registered with Central Casting as general extras, courtesy of the Queen. They had signed their names at one wicket and stood half-blinded by the camera flash for their identity file photos. Without the influence of the Queen of the Extras, Frankie and Connie wouldn't have a hope of starting in the movies today.

"Frankie, will you cheer up and start enjoying yourself?" Connie hissed as they hurried along, the Queen at their heels.

"I'll try." Because they were *here*. In Monument Studios, ready to report for their *first day* as extras in the movie business. With these italicized thoughts she tried to drum a proper excitement into the moment, but the memory of that dead white hand weighed on her like lead-lined luggage.

Frankie pinched the webbing below each of her thumbs — an old trick of hers when she wanted to concentrate — as they rounded the corner to the outdoor area where a crowd of extras milled noisily about. Among them Frankie identified Doris by her honey-coloured hair. She scanned the buzzing, cigarette-puffing crowd for Tom's blue sweater. She had looked right past him twice before she saw that although he was still wearing his usual sweater, he was also sporting a white skirt patterned with red cherries. He wore a flowered scarf around his head, with a few curls teased out. He met her startled look with a mischievous, lipsticked grin.

The Queen called Tom over. "How late are we, kiddo? Have these girls missed a shot?"

"You haven't missed a thing." He adjusted the tie of his head-scarf. "We're waiting on the assistant director. He's late. As per usual. What are *you* dolls staring at?"

Connie laughed. "Look who's calling who a *doll*."

Frankie asked, "Is this what you mean by *dressing* up for the scene?"

"You bet your bottom dollar." Tom swished his skirt. "This picture's set in wartime Paris. The young men are off fighting, so casting wants old men and young girls for the scene. Either I'm a girl, or I don't work."

"It's all par for the course around here. I don't even have to apply his mascara for him anymore," the Queen said. "Tom, I'm due at Paramount for the voodoo scene. Look after these girls, will you?"

"I'll defend them with my very life," Tom said. "I'll lay me doon and *dee*."

The Queen kissed his closely shaved cheek. "And listen hard for what's new in studio gossip, all of you. Ask questions. We need seven new items of interest for Blanche's Tuesday column by this Sunday night." The Queen looked closely at Frankie's face. "Frankie, are you sure nothing's the matter?"

Frankie bit her lip. "I'm fine."

The Queen laid her palm against Frankie's forehead, as if checking for fever. "You look like you've seen a ghost."

"Do I?" Frankie tried her eyebrows up and then down. She quirked the corners of her mouth. "Better?"

"No." The Queen patted Frankie's cheek. "That's not acting, dear, that's mugging. I never guessed you for the nervous type."

"She's doing her best," Connie said.

"Look, if I miss the voodoo night scene at Paramount, I'll be snookered." The Queen slapped Tom across the shoulder. "Cheer this Frankie girl up."

"I'll tell her jokes," Tom said. "I'll tickle her toes."

Frankie stood between Connie and Tom and watched the older woman walk away.

Nobody should have to deal with seeing a dead hand on her first day of work.

"Will you for crow's sake tell us what's wrong with you?" Connie demanded.

Frankie gave in and told them about the body in the backyard. It was difficult to get the words out—they wanted to stick in her mouth like dry biscuits. "Eugene said the dead fellow would be somebody poor, who couldn't afford a funeral."

"And you *touched* the dead man's fingers? I wouldn't do it if you paid me." Connie exchanged a look with Tom. "Would *you* bury your old uncle in somebody's backyard?"

"Maybe, if there was nowhere else to put him." Tom shook his head. "It's a lean year. A funeral might set you back a couple hundred bucks. I'm sorry, Frankie, but you have got to rise above it. It's only the assistant director today, but it's better to go home sick than foul out. He already thinks we're a herd of untalented cattle."

"*She* can do it. Frankie's ready for anything," Connie said. Frankie nodded.

In Frankie's ear, Connie asked, "Are you really all right? Do you want to go home?"

"I'm better. Thanks." She shivered as Tom pointed out the extra's toilet block. Across from her, a line of extras—wearing, like Frankie, Connie, and Tom, ordinary women's day clothes—waited outside a storage shed for a cup of coffee served from a trolley by a gentleman wearing an apron. A small boy with a cigar hanging out of the corner of his mouth stood nearby, a cup of coffee in one hand and a sandwich in the other. Frankie watched as the boy contemplated his sandwich. Smoke drifted to the brim of his school cap, divided, and drifted upward. The smell of it made her want to throw up.

Connie frowned. "You're shaking, kid."

"Don't keep talking about it," Frankie begged. Thank heavens it was only the assistant director working with the extras today. The only way she could have been luckier would be if it was the assistant to the assistant director. She peered at the lineup beside the coffee trolley. She wished they would serve the extras cocoa instead, or tea. "Why is that child smoking?"

"Hey, Bruno, why are you smoking?" Tom called to the boy.

"It's a free country," the boy growled. But of course he wasn't a boy at all, Frankie saw, just a very small man in his twenties, close-shaven, wearing a schoolboy's cap and short pants and smoking a well-used cigar. Tom said, "Do you recognize him? Bruno used to be a child star in the single reels."

"The big time." Bruno grinned. "Now look at me, just an extra."

"Gosh." To Tom, who was dressed as a woman, Frankie murmured, "Nothing is as it seems in Hollywood."

Above them, palm trees lined the studio wall. Around and about, a series of sheds and crates provided shadowed seats for at least fifty more extras, a carefree brigade of men and women chatting over cups of coffee and smokes.

"How about a sandwich?" Connie asked. "I'll get you one."

"I'm not hungry, thanks," Frankie answered, but Connie pressed a sandwich on her anyway. Cheese. That was good. If it had been tomato, she wouldn't be able to slip it into her pocket for later, as she did now.

Through a gap between the buildings, she spotted a camera — no, two — like the one Leo had brought to the Vancouver audition. In the centre of an open space stood a weather-darkened bronze statue of a soldier astride a horse. Even from this distance, she observed that the horse had three feet on the ground and one raised, as if to advance across the square. All in all, the square looked to Frankie's eye quite believably Parisian. In the shadows of a pillared façade that looked as if it were meant to play the part of a bank, two men in fedoras stood head to head, jutting their chins at an argumentative tilt. It reminded her of Leo and Gilbert Howard, which in turn reminded her of the way Connie had frozen in front of the camera. She mustn't allow that to happen again.

"Say," Frankie asked Tom, "do any of these professionals know how to deal with a case of camera shyness?"

She caught the pointy end of Connie's look and added quickly, "It happens to me sometimes." She whispered in Connie's ear, "For Pete's sake, I'm not about to tell anybody it happened to *you.*"

"It was just the one time," Connie hissed back.

"Girls, there's one thing you can get for free in this town, and that's advice." Tom waved a crowd of other extras over and spread their names around until Frankie was thoroughly confused.

"Camera shyness?" Doris chewed on the rim of her paper cup. "I know a girl who beat it through breathing. Count to ten, and then puff into a paper bag." She put her hand to her belly and sucked in the air loudly.

"Okay. Like this?" Frankie sucked in her breath and Connie followed suit.

A grey-haired fellow in a pinstriped jacket piped up, "Freezing up in front of the camera is simply a result of lack of preparation. As professionals, you must learn your lines."

"We don't have any lines," Tom pointed out. "We're *extras.*"

"Gilbert Howard forgets his lines all the time these days," a young woman in blue said. "And nobody kicks Howard off the lot when he starts spouting Shakespeare instead of his real lines in the middle of a speakeasy scene."

A professional argument developed between Doris and the man in the pinstriped jacket.

"You people have missed the mark," an elderly man in rusty black interrupted. "The trick is to communicate with the audience, to imagine their support, as if you were on stage and could feel their presence in the dark."

"Really?" Connie asked. "That sounds so complicated."

"*Booze.* There's your mother courage." Bruno shifted his cigar from one side of his mouth to the other, reached into the back pocket of his schoolboy trousers, and pulled out a leather-covered flask.

"*What* were they all again?" Connie looked from one extra to another, blinked, and counted on her fingers.

But she was too late. One of the two chin-jutting arguers wearing fedoras and long raincoats stepped into the waiting area. He barked, "All right, girls and boys, we're ready for the take."

"The assistant director," Doris explained.

"From his crooked toes to his pointed head," Bruno added.

Frankie's legs felt heavy. Her throat was dry. On the positive side, though, her knees were steady. Around her, she sensed a rustle of professional reluctance, as if the extras were soldiers rallied to the front. The crowd dropped sandwich ends and cigarette butts into paper cups, set them down in the gravel around the storage shacks, and made their way onto the set. They stood in a bunch in the middle of the square, between the statue and the bank building.

The assistant director took off his fedora and scratched a bald spot. "Listen, you lugs. You're meant to gather in this here square in groupings of two or threes, and walk where we showed you already. No mugging for attention. Do what you're paid for. And you—yeah, *you*, Bruno the Kid—try to look like you didn't slit your mother's throat."

At Frankie's side, Bruno muttered, "The only way I'd get less respect is if I were a woman." A snicker rippled through the extras nearest him.

"Shut up. And by the way," the director's assistant added, "anybody looks at the camera, I'll personally remove both your eyes."

"Charming," a pretty girl in purple laughed. Her hair was damp but combed, and her dress stuck to her in several places.

"You—put some underwear on next time," the assistant director snapped. "And walk behind somebody today. Only stars have nipples, kid."

The girl in purple pulled a moue. The extras moved onto the set.

"Here, take the car keys," Connie whispered. "I don't want anything spoiling the line of my dress. And give me that sandwich, will you? I want to make a wish. Like on a turkey wishbone."

Frankie dropped the keys to the car and the bungalow into her left pocket and pulled her uneaten cheese sandwich out of her right. Connie took hold of one side of it and pulled it in two. Frankie stared at the smaller portion that was left in her hand.

"I'm making a wish." Connie closed her eyes for a second and then opened them wide. "Frankie, the wish came true. We're in the movies."

"Don't bet on it," Bruno said from behind them. "Like as not, we'll all end up on the cutting room floor."

"Either way, we're on film." Frankie put the rest of the sandwich back into her pocket. She held out her unsteady left hand and Connie pressed her palm against it. "For luck."

Connie held tight to Frankie's arm. They followed Tom, Bruno, and the other extras across the square. The assistant director jerked his thumb up. Did that mean the cameras were rolling, or was this a rehearsal? She supposed that it didn't matter. She'd do her best either way. She and Connie walked around the statue of the soldier on his horse. Frankie felt more like an awkward automaton than an actress, so to add a little realism and to keep from looking at the camera, she gazed up at the mighty horse. At close quarters, Frankie made sure that it was not cast in bronze but in painted plaster. She wondered what her father would say if he could see her right now on this movie sound stage. Probably he'd say, *Frankie, when a statue horse has four feet on the ground, it means the rider died in bed. Three legs on the ground means wounded in combat.* Like he hadn't told her a thousand times. *When the horse has two legs off the ground, it means the rider died in battle.*

"Act like I'm talking to you, Connie," she suggested. They walked arm and arm like the schoolgirls they had recently been, across to the edge of the square. There, Connie stumbled a little on a flowerbed made of brown burlap.

"Cut," the assistant director called. For a terrible moment, Frankie feared he had cut the take because of Connie's error. But no voices were raised, and Connie was not picked out of the crowd, so they must not have noticed. Around the square, cameramen chewed gum and leaned on their cameras.

"Anyway, I didn't freeze," Connie hissed. "Was the camera on me when I tripped?"

"I don't know. After the assistant director's threat, I was looking everywhere except at the camera. Anyway, people trip in real life. I think it's a good bit of business." Frankie squeezed Connie's shoulder. "There! We're on film. *Klahowya.*"

"*Klahowya.*" They grinned at each other.

Frankie would later remember this as the last carefree moment of her young life before everything changed.

From the left, somebody shouted, "*You.*"

Connie turned. "Who?"

"*That* one." Across the lot, a woman in a bright red dress shaded her face with one hand. Marietta Valdes carried her shoes by their slender straps. She walked barefoot past the assistant director toward the extras. She was joined by a man in black Frankie had never seen before. On Marietta's other side strode King Samson.

Frankie had a craven impulse to run and hide. She braced herself with the thought that she was just an extra in a group of extras. They were all doing their jobs, professionally and above board. The other extras appeared to have no keen interest in Marietta Valdes the movie star, or even in the producer, King Samson. No, it was the man in black who drew all eyes. The extras turned to him like sunflowers to the light.

Frankie had seen the man in black's picture in the movie magazines. She knew him at once for the director. Her heart filled with a sensation that was not exactly new, but one she had never before identified. It was the feeling that an important moment loomed, and that a turning point approached. Simply by standing here, listening to the director and participating in the making of a film, she was poised atop the fulcrum around which the world turned. She might be nobody, but she was in the movies. She couldn't wish for anything more, she thought, wishing all the while for a real live part. She wondered whether the others — Connie, Tom, Doris, Bruno, and the rest — felt the same.

"You," the director said. He nodded to Connie as she stood at Frankie's side. "Come here. I want to use you in a shot."

Connie caught one hand with the other and held them tight to her middle. She stepped forward.

Frankie whispered, "I *knew* they'd pick you."

An angel out of a row of kewpie dolls, that's what they said about Marietta Valdes. And now they'd say it about Connie.

The director shook his head. "Not you. *You*. You, with the sorrowful phiz."

Connie stepped back uncertainly. Frankie pushed Connie forward again.

"Are you deaf? Not the redhead." The director was waving both hands. "*You*, the sad sack. The pale and mournful brunette. You're the one I want."

Connie stepped back. Director, star, extras, and cameramen—everybody stared at Frankie. To her horror, she found herself shifting uncomfortably from one foot to the other. Shifting weight was the certain identifying mark of the amateur actor.

She held herself still.

It was the strangest thing: standing barefaced and alone in front of the director caused her peripheral vision to blur and her concentration to narrow to the point where she could hold only one thought at a time. The rest of her mind, the unused bits, felt as if she'd wrapped them up in greyish batting and put them in a bottom bureau drawer. She did her best to concentrate on the director's scowling face.

Frankie blurted out, "What would you like me to do?" There was something wrong with that sentence. She added, "Sir?"

One of the extras laughed. There was a shifting sound, as if from a crowd of grass-skirted kewpie dolls. Behind the extras, the back of King Samson's camel-coloured coat flew out behind him as he stormed off the set.

THE BIRTHDAY PARTY

Melisa Gregorio

Melisa Gregorio's *fiction has appeared in* Pearls, Ricepaper, *and elsewhere. She is completing a collection of short stories and revising her first novel. In addition to being a writer, Melisa works as a master's-prepared registered nurse specializing in education and clinical informatics.*

The Birthday Party

Even at nine years old, Ashley was the type who knew and used our teacher's first name. "Irene," she whispered to us. We repeated it among ourselves, the name as forbidden as a swear word. On the day of Ashley's birthday party, the eight of us lined up outside her house. We poked each other and dared one another to ring the doorbell. When someone finally lifted a hand toward the door, it was opened by Ashley's mom. Our feet were already too big for the tsinelas she offered us, but after we took off our rain jackets and boots, we shoved our feet into the jewelled slippers.

In the living room, we saw Ashley bouncing from couch to couch. The plastic coverings made her slip with every jump. Balloons were scattered across the floor, bobbing up and down as if afraid to land on the carpet.

Instead of saying hi, Ashley leapt off a couch onto a balloon. Pop! Immediately, we started jumping on the balloons, causing a gunfire of pops. We had dropped our gifts to join the fun, and there was a sudden silence when Ashley picked up a present and opened it. How dare she? We stood, frozen—everyone knew it was food, cake, games, *then* presents, goody bags, home.

This breach of party etiquette was typical of Ashley: she did what she wanted.

Ashley unwrapped the gift to reveal *Little Women.* "What a waste of money," she said, and dropped the book. "We have this in the library."

The shocked silence continued. Ashley picked up another present, but dropped it when her mom came in from the kitchen. On the living room table, she set down platters of lumpia and pancit. "Come eat! It's no good cold," she said. Everyone grabbed a plate and helped themselves to spring rolls and noodles. Ashley didn't eat, but instead sat cross-legged on the couch.

We finished eating and carried our plates to the kitchen. Ashley's mother asked if we were ready for cake. We nodded and returned to the living room, only to see Ashley was gone.

Her mother called her daughter to the table. When Ashley didn't appear, we searched for her. We looked behind the couches, in the kitchen, and in the closets. We were too shy to open the closed doors we knew were bedrooms.

"That bad girl! Running away again," her mother muttered. "Please," she said, "look outside?"

We threw on our jackets and boots. Outside it was raining, and we ran down the slick driveway. We heard a shout and saw Ashley waving to us from the top of the hill. She was on her bike and wore her dad's motorcycle helmet. It had an opaque visor, and we couldn't see her face. She crouched down and pumped her legs furiously, speeding down the hill. Some kids, like Ashley, rode on the street. Other kids, like us, rode on the sidewalk. After that day, Ashley didn't ride at all.

We jumped up and down, cheering for Ashley, and even the rain landing on the neighbours' parked cars sounded liked applause for her. Our shouts blurred in our ears. At sleepovers, to parents, in therapy, we would cry and ask: did we distract Ashley? If we hadn't been cheering so loud that day, would she have seen the Dodge Ramcharger reversing out of the driveway? Could she have stopped in time and then, with her characteristic panache, kicked the Dodge's tires while yelling at the driver? Ashley would have finished biking down the hill, and we would have gone back into her house to sing 'Happy Birthday'. We would have eaten cake and played games. Holding our goody bags, we would have been picked up and would have had the fun of talking over the party on the phone that night.

But Ashley — because of our screams? — didn't see the SUV backing up. She tried to brake, but it was too late. Her bike slammed into the vehicle, and Ashley went over her handlebars, the velocity causing her too-big motorcycle helmet to fly off. Her unprotected head struck the rear window, spiderwebbing the glass. The impact caused her brain to bounce back and forth inside her skull, crushing, ripping, and shearing her delicate brain tissue.

Her mother pushed past us and ran up the road to her daughter's broken body. She screamed at us to call 9-1-1 and pushed down on Ashley's chest. Even from where we stood, we heard the snap of her ribs. Her mother paused, her hands hovering, but then continued her CPR, repeating "Ashley" like a prayer. With each compression, bright red blood leaked out of her daughter's mouth.

The teenaged driver of the Ramcharger knelt beside Ashley and screamed, "I didn't see her! She came out of nowhere!"

We watched the CPR and listened to the teenager's sobs. Wet and numb, we stood silent, even after the ambulance came and left. When our parents arrived, they found us in the pouring rain, unable to move. No one knew what to say. How could we explain what had happened when that meant explaining Ashley? How could we begin to explain who she was, and who she was to us?

None of us went to the funeral; none of us were invited. A few weeks later, our birthday presents to Ashley were returned to us, along with her funeral service card. But unlike our parents, who refused to say her name — as if tragedy were contagious — we said it to each other, to ourselves. While our teacher's name, Irene, had been a compliment or an insult depending on our mood, Ashley's name became our sacred mantra. We whispered "Ashley" the first time we rode our bikes after the birthday party; as we shoplifted our first pair of heels; the moment after the condom was unwrapped; and when we had daughters of our own. We both feared and hoped our girls would be just like Ashley.

WATERSHAKERS

Christi Nogle

Christi Nogle's short stories have appeared in publications such as
PseudoPod, Escape Pod, Vastarien, *and* Tales to Terrify.
Follow her at christinogle.com or on Twitter @christinogle.

Watershakers

Mom screamed at me to do something about the horse trough. When I went out there, the mosquito larvae's herky-jerky dance hypnotized me. Algae, seedpods, and grass floated on the surface.

I considered pouring in some bleach, but that's no good for horses. I imagined suck-starting a hose, imagined the horses dancing around, all joyous to have clean water. The idea of sucking that water grossed me out, though. I didn't see a hose right away. Then I got distracted. The horses don't mind running down to the creek if they get thirsty, anyway.

By the time I came around again, the water was low and dark. I thought, *I really do have to do something about this.* The larvae were doing more of a belly dance now, sinuous hip shakes instead of the jerk. I lifted out a handful of water and saw three little transparent women rolling their hips in my palm. I just about screamed. Even as I held them, two slowed and stopped moving. The centre one kept on.

She was clear like mineral jelly, her skeleton built like a human's but made of silver wire, her pale organs more or less like ours, as far as I knew.

A jelly head but no face, no skull, a little pink brain floating on its stem.

I dropped her in a big tumbler of water on my nightstand. She stood and moved her hips in swift circles again. I watched — too long. When I returned, Mom had managed to tip over the trough. I cried seeing what all was scattered on the ground.

The one in my water glass seemed to be all right, though. She twitched and twitched her imaginary hula hoop all that night. I woke up several times to flick on the lamp and check her. I knew she needed food because she was moving more and more slowly each time, and by morning she jerked barely at all.

I guessed they'd been eating algae and leaves, but every pet I'd had has loved raw hamburger, so that's what I tried. I impaled a ball of meat on a toothpick and lowered it down to her. The blood aura wafted toward her head, which stretched up to meet it. I imagined what would happen: the dimple in the top of her head would deepen to engulf the meat and suck it into a throat that opened above her collarbone.

I didn't get to stay and watch. I had chores, school. When I returned, she'd grown an inch and shook at full speed. I thought she must be happy.

She was half as tall as a Barbie when I got to thinking how her skeleton wasn't all the way finished, how she had no skull. Maybe there was some deficiency. Minerals? I took the tumbler to the trough. She leaped out and swam to the rusted edge. Her head opened and took in a large flake of metal. She came back to the tumbler and shook her hips like, *OK, let's go home.*

After that I fed her screws and staples along with the hamburger, which really helped. Her skeleton grew sturdier, and a little chrome skull began to grow. I watched it form — as much as I could since I was busy with school and chores. It started as thin as a spider's web, like a fine-line pencil sketch. Day by day, the lines grew wider, until one day she had a perfect skull with perfect little silver teeth. It had all the cool of a heavy metal album cover. The clear jelly outside the skull formed a pleasant profile, too: upturned nose, sharp chin. She would have been pretty if she'd had skin.

Her movements enthralled me. I imagined sitting on the bathtub's edge and sliding in to dance with a full-grown version of her. I was afraid, though. Her jelly might sting. Her head might open again.

Or I might harm her.

She had to squat now to stay submerged in the tumbler. I was feeding her stranger and stranger things — lint and blood, fingernails, hair — and at night I had terrible dreams. This couldn't continue.

I knew I would release her in water, but I couldn't see her being happy in a river, and I couldn't get her to the sea. I settled on the neighbour's dark, smelly pond. Fish to eat, if she grew large enough. If not, snails and insects.

I felt stupid carrying the Kool-Aid pitcher, relieved I didn't run into anyone on the way. Once there, I pushed the pitcher down into pond water before I could change my mind.

She lay, shaking her hips in the shallows. Suddenly she tensed, plunged her arm into mud, and pulled out a worm. She held it up like she was saying *Victory!* She slurped the wriggling thing, then jerked her head toward something else. She bolted into the depths. I couldn't see her anymore.

I tucked big stones around the pitcher so it wouldn't float away. I thought if she got homesick, she might go back, or maybe I just didn't want to carry it home.

I was awfully sad, walking away. It was like when we put Sam to sleep, or the night we got the call about Dad. Everything lost.

The pitcher was still there the first couple of times I visited, and then it was gone.

I got back to routine: Mom screaming about chores, me being distracted, video games, a field trip to the state capitol. Things really were normal by the time I thought of her again. I was at a friend's house watching a movie where a woman was giving a lap dance on a dare. I couldn't look away. The woman's upturned nose and her grinding motions took me back to all those hours watching the little watershaker behind the glass.

I went out to the pond that night, expecting to mope around the edges like before, but something moved in a group of scrubby trees across the water. I approached.

Her chrome teeth flashed in moonlight. She was chewing a great big frog, legs sticking out of her mouth, skin and blood on her lips.

When she saw me, she stood her full six feet and shimmied—in greeting, I suppose. I was proud to see silver hairs starting on her head and new marbled skin, like the skin of a plum frosted over with blue. I could still see through to her organs, but just barely.

Was she full-grown? I couldn't say. I didn't think so.

I reached toward her, and she shuddered back a few feet. She squatted there a while and ran her fingers in the mud, looking up at me every so often. Then she jumped up, went behind a tree, and came back, offering the pitcher. I smiled and handed it back. *It's yours to keep.*

She misunderstood. She went down to the pond's edge and filled it with water. She offered it again. I didn't take it.

She shimmied slowly. She looked inside the pitcher and shimmied at the same time. When I took it, she went down on all fours and slid into the pond.

Right up till then, I'd been thinking how we were really connecting, but maybe she didn't feel the same. She didn't swim back, didn't surface. I started to get sad, but then I noticed something.

The pitcher vibrated in my hands.

It kept shaking as I walked home. I couldn't wait to shine a light into the water. I'd see silver women, surely, but in my imagination there were little golden men in there too, jewelled horses, dragons in red and in green.

PULP
Literature
Good books for the price of a beer
Allaigna's Song Overture JM Landels
PULP Literature
Short stories, poetry, and comics you can't put down
www.pulpliterature.com

THE SAFEST PLACE IN A TRAILER DURING A TORNADO IS THE BATHTUB

Patti Jeane Pangborn

Patti Jeane Pangborn *is a PhD candidate in English with a concentration in Creative Writing at the University of Louisiana at Lafayette. Her poetry has been published in* OCCULUM, The Lab Review, Soul-Lit, *and the* Columbia Poetry Review. *Patti's chapbook,* ADRIFT, *available from Space Cowboy Books, features a lonely astronaut who pines for Earth. She is the co-editor-in-chief of* Rougarou: Journal of Arts and Literature. *Her dissertation examines the occult poetics of WB Yeats, Jack Spicer, and CAConrad.*

The Safest Place in a Trailer During a Tornado Is the Bathtub

The landscape of home has lost its gravity.   Stones float up from

the driveway   the pine and birch branches bend and stretch

their snapping echoes   the windows blown out glass   suspended   curtains

reaching after the shards   the German plates and doilies   my school pictures

in their frames   cracked and smiling   my mother's open jewellery box sails lazily out

her bedroom window trailing   my baby teeth   my father's watch   his wedding ring.

The metal roof begins to give   opening on one side like a hinge and I

see birds' nests made of my rust-stained hair glide by   feel the floor of the trailer

begin to rise   its skirt lifting in metallic squeals as the eye of my dream shudders past.

DEEP WATER

Mike Carson

Mike Carson has been teaching high school English for thirty years, and, like many other English teachers, he has been working on a novel for approximately the same length of time: it's going to be great. Mike lives in Kamloops with his wife, fledgling twin sons, and an eclectic assortment of ill-mannered pets. 'Deep Water' was a runner-up for the 2019 Surrey International Writers' Conference Storyteller Award, judged by Jack Whyte and Diana Gabaldon.

Deep Water

I could hear my father shouting as I passed the nurses' station. Room 1201A: portal to Hell. I tried to pump a little iron into my spine as I pushed through the heavy faux-wood door. Everything in the room was pretty much as it had been on my last visit, including the shouting: the same seasickness-green walls, scuffed by the rubber bumpers of countless hospital beds. In the humid air, the smell of stale urine and industrial cleanser were duking it out. As usual, urine had the upper hand.

The curtain was open on the old man's side of the room, his bed neatly made, a hospital cart on wheels rolled up to it. There was a small television mounted on a swivel arm — ten bucks extra per day for that little luxury, by the way — a small table, yellow flowers withering in a vase, an IV cart, and the usual hospital machinery that could make all variety of pings and beeps and buzzes but could do nothing to bring back an old man's mind.

I stepped around the curtain toward the little sitting area: a barred window with two rocking chairs overlooking a vista of flat rooftops and air-conditioning units. In the distance, two scraggly palm trees clawed at the smoggy California skyline. The old man stood in front of the window, arms waving, obscenities pouring out of his mouth. His hospital gown was untied at the back, white ass-cheeks protruding like two plastic bags filled with cottage cheese. Charlie Cahill: A bare, forked animal, an unaccommodated man. My old man.

The brunt of his wrath was borne, as usual, by Rose Celestin, a young Haitian nurse with long, glistening hair twisted into tight cornrows. She was standing with her arms folded across her narrow chest, head tilted to one side. She looked as fragile as a bird, but I'd seen her toss these old-timers around like they were bags of cotton candy. "Mr Cahill," she said, "why don't you go on and get yourself dressed?" She pointed at a pile of neatly folded clothes on the table beside her. "You'll need your medicine before dinner. They'll be missing you in the dining room."

"Who the hell are you?" he said, pointing a bony finger. "You're the bitch that's been stealin' from me, ain'tcha?" He turned toward the door, saw me. "Wally," he said, squinting, "That's you, ain't it? Call the cops, Wally. They're stealin' from me."

Wally. His brother. Killed over fifty years ago, back in '68, just outside Da Nang. The old man told me once that what they shipped home of Wally could have been buried in a cereal box. "No, Dad," I said. "I'm Matt, your son. Remember?"

His shoulders fell. He began to shake, and tears trickled out of the corners of his eyes. "Liar," he said quietly. "My son's dead." He turned, giving me a full view of everything he didn't have on, and then sat down in one of the rockers. He stared straight ahead, not moving, as if he could see to the end of the world. Or maybe it was only the palm trees.

"Bonswa, Matthew," Rose said, putting a little French twist on my name so that it sounded a bit like a classy sneeze: *Mah-choo.*

"Tough day?" I said.

She shrugged.

I walked to the old man, put my hand on his shoulder. "Hey Dad," I said. "Gonna get dressed today?"

"Fuck off, Wally," he said. He started to rock, still staring straight ahead. His shoulders were shaking. Whose wouldn't, I thought, if your dead brother's ghost kept dropping by to visit?

"Where the hell's Maria?" he said.

Maria. His wife. Dead since 1980 — three years after I was born. I knew her from pictures and a single, bright shard of memory: green and red lights framing the face of a smiling, dark-haired lady who held me in her arms. The smell of cigarettes and vanilla. Nothing more.

"She couldn't make it," I said.

The old man stood up. When he turned to face me his eyes were wide, frightened. "Go get Maria, Wally. I need Maria. She'll know what to do." He put his hands to his head, squeezed. "Something's wrong with me." He dropped his hands again, leaving a few tufts of white hair sticking straight up from the top of his head like some demented prophet.

"He need his meds," Rose said.

"Okay," I said. "You take these pills, and I'll bring Maria tomorrow." It made me feel like shit, lying to him. I'd told him about a dozen times that his wife was long dead, and each time he would weep as though she'd died that day. My old man, crying. In all the years I'd known him, he rarely cracked a smile, never shed a tear, and now the wrong kind of Jell-O at dinner could reduce him to mush.

Rose and I managed to get the old man to swallow the pills — he was convinced they were poison but took them anyway. Maybe he was hoping for poison.

I helped him into some clothes. He fought every step of the way. "Dinner time," Rose said. "Comin', Matthew?"

"Would it make any difference?"

"Course it would," she said, turning to look straight in my face—in a manner I felt was a little accusatory, considering who was paying the bills around here—"You be spendin' time with your papa."

"He thinks I'm a ghost. Ghosts and dinner don't mix: ever read *Macbeth*?"

She let that slide. "The doctor, he say he want talk with you."

"When?"

"'Round seven. You stay till then?"

"Sure."

We helped the old man into a wheelchair. He wouldn't look at me. "Takin' me to the gas chamber," he said. He didn't sound disappointed.

"Dinner," I said. "Bet it's meatloaf. I'll be here when you get back."

Rose wheeled the old man away, and I sat down in one of the rockers, alone with the sunset, the smell of piss, and the heavy weight of time. From behind me came the soft hiss of oxygen from Mr Schwartz's half of the room. My father's roommate—he had to be at least ninety—was riding an induced coma straight to oblivion. His daughter had stopped visiting a month ago: what they hadn't said to one another by now would never be said, I suppose.

I took out my phone and texted the kid: *Visiting Gramps. Be home late. I'll bring burgers.*

A while later he texted back: *How's G-Dawg?*

Still nuts. How was school?

No reply. Apparently the conversation was over. *Good talk, son. CU later.*

His mother had named him Atticus. I said it was a hipster name, so, now that she had dumped her portion of the parenting duties on me, I called him Finch. It had started as a joke — or maybe just something to piss her off — but the name suited him. He was fourteen, pale, scrawny, with long, unruly black hair and his mother's angular features: narrow, sharp nose and furtive black eyes. He had started wearing a leather jacket at least two sizes too big for him, and thrift shop T-shirts with the logos of bands like Slayer and Megadeth on them. I hated the jacket most of all: it was like a black void swallowing up my son.

He went out on weekends, and came home smelling of whiskey, pot, and puke. I once spent twenty minutes trying to remove bloodstains from his favourite Black Sabbath shirt. When he finally stumbled out of bed, trying to hide the shiners behind a pair of dark glasses, I asked him what happened.

"A little misunderstanding," he said.

A little misunderstanding. Christ. I'm in so far over my head, I don't know which way is up.

Rose rolled the old man in earlier than usual. It turned out dinner had to be cut short because Charlie had started throwing food around and accusing all the Jews of stealing his watch. They had to sedate him: he was riding the Haldol Highway now.

I helped Rose take him to the toilet and then lift him into bed. "I'm sorry," I said.

"Don't apologize for your papa," she said. "It's not who he really is."

I shrugged. "What if it is? What if …" I couldn't finish the sentence, acknowledge that maybe Charlie Cahill had always been mean, racist, angry; that maybe, at the last, the veneer of civility had been stripped away and what remained was the unvarnished truth of the man. "I don't know how you do it," I said.

Rose moved closer. "In my country," she said, "the spirits of the dead are all 'round us. In the deep water." She touched the old man's shoulder. "I think people like your papa, they in between this world and the next. They scared, confused. They can see the deep water, what's down there. But when we cross over, when we lost and scared, they guide us."

Faith, I thought. Another opiate. Still, there was something glimmering in Rose's eyes that was too pure to extinguish with logic. "So you think there's a point to all of this?" I said, waving my hands to indicate the shabby hospital room, the withered old man on the bed. "To suffering?"

"That's how you know you still alive," she said.

I didn't feel like plunging any further into the existential vortex of this conversation, so I said, "Sounds fair."

Rose smiled. "I see all kinds in here," she said. "You're a good son, Matthew."

The words stung a bit.

She turned to the door. "See you later?"

"Later. And thanks again," I said, but she was gone.

I looked down at the old man: the wispy, grey hair, the atrophying musculature; skin so thin you could trace the veins below the surface. A sagging sack of flesh clinging to life, autonomic functions slavishly performing their duties, machine-like, as the mind decayed. I could end his suffering: a pillow over the face, stop the breath. Easeful death. I'd never do it, of course. Maybe because it's wrong — or maybe because I'm a coward. "You won't go gentle into that good night, will you, Dad?" I said.

Behold your Divine Justice.

Over forty years of laying bricks, pouring concrete, working until arthritis clawed his hands, bowed his back, bent his knees. He'd done his best to raise me by himself after Mom died. There was nothing I could hold against him, we just never really saw things eye to eye. We'd been staring each other down for years over Christmas hams and Thanksgiving turkeys. If it weren't for Finch, I probably wouldn't have seen him even then.

At sixty-five he retired to finally enjoy his reward for a lifetime of work: early-onset Alzheimer's. It was manageable at first: he'd forget his phone number, or his address, or to eat, but, with a little home support, he got by. But Alzheimer's is merciless, and the inevitable conclusion of Charlie Cahill's eventful history would be him gasping his last breath in palliative care in the nursing home at Our Lady of Perpetual Atonement.

I'd had to sell his house, of course. His medical insurance wasn't nearly enough to cover the four-grand-per-month hospital bill, and his life savings would soon be gone. Between alimony and rent, my community college teaching salary was already stretched past the breaking point. Another year of this, and we'd all be out on the street. At least Charlie wouldn't notice the change of scenery.

My pity party was interrupted by the arrival of Dr Muller, a round, amiable man pushing sixty with a penchant for plaid, short-sleeved dress shirts and loafers. He'd been treating the old man for years. "How's your dad, Matt?" he said.

"You tell me," I said.

He flicked the switch for the overhead light. The fluorescents hummed to life. Muller looked at his clipboard. "We ran some tests today," he said. "I'm afraid it's not good news."

No surprise there. He handed me the clipboard. "You're familiar with the clock-drawing test?"

"Sure." We'd been through it hundreds of times: the patient is asked to draw a clock displaying the time 2:45. I looked at the clipboard. "He drew this one today?"

Muller nodded. The clock in the picture was a disaster: the face was teardrop shaped, not round, and the numbers were out of sequence, stacked up along each side. The hands were curved, and both the same length, like a horseshoe. "So he's getting better?" I said.

Muller smiled. "It's good to keep a sense of humour."

"It's all I can afford."

"Your father's symptoms are typical of late-phase Stage 6 dementia. At Stage 7, most patients suffer rapid, severe cognitive deterioration, and are incapable of speech and, in most cases, movement without assistance. There is no treatment, of course, save making the patient as comfortable as possible."

"How long?"

"Typically, no more than thirty months; however, your father has been experiencing a number of small strokes, almost daily, that are accelerating his decline. I can't be more definitive than that." He shrugged. "Of course, there's always hope to cling to."

"I'm already treading water," I said. I sat down and ran my fingers through my hair. "Jesus, doc, I don't want to sound like an asshole, but I don't know how I can pay for this." I looked up, "What's the going rate for a forty-two-year-old kidney nowadays?"

"About a quarter-million," he said, deadpan.

"You're a riot, doc, you know that?"

"I understand the financial burden that terminal illness can place on families," he said, "but there are options."

"Apart from selling my organs?"

"Yes. Let's keep that as a last resort." He laughed. "There's someone I'd like you to meet. Naturally, I haven't discussed any specific details of your father's case. I'll leave that up to you." He went to the door. "Please come in, Ms Cornwall."

With a clacking of heels not unlike the sound of hooves on brimstone, Ms Cornwall clattered into the room. She might have been thirty or sixty: auburn hair drawn back into a meticulous French roll, a few strategically loosened strands framing a heart-shaped face that tapered gracefully toward a pointed chin. She wore wire-rimmed glasses that made her grey eyes appear unnaturally large and liquid, and her dark wool pantsuit and close-toed pumps screamed corporate shill. It occurred to me the moment I shook her cool, dry hand that I might be tempted to sell something more precious than a kidney.

"It's a pleasure to meet you, Mr Cahill," she said.

"That's Mr Cahill," I said, pointing to the old man on the bed. "Matt."

"Matt, then," she said. "Please call me Regan."

"I'll leave the two of you to chat," Muller said, edging toward the door. "Plenty more patients to see tonight. I'll be in touch."

"What's this about?" I said.

"It may be better to discuss this somewhere else. Can I buy you a cup of coffee?"

Seated in the industrial glare of the hospital cafeteria, two overpriced cups of tepid Sanka before us, Ms Cornwall began her pitch: "Although I don't know all of the details of your family situation," she said, "I do understand the tremendous pressures, both financial and emotional, that you are facing. I represent a company that I think may be able to help."

She placed a matte-black business card on the dingy table. The name 'Weltgeist' was embossed at the top, accompanied by a small logo depicting an androgynous figure holding a globe. In smaller letters at the bottom: 'Regan Cornwall, Public Relations and Marketing', along with her contact information.

"I'll admit I need help," I said, "but I'm sorry. I just don't understand."

"At this moment," she said, "what is it that you need most?"

"Money," I said.

She shook her head, took a sip of coffee, grimaced. "Money is an issue, of course, but we can always borrow money, earn more money. Try again."

I thought about all the things I had to do: I was losing Finch, that was certain, I was way behind at work — my last evaluation had not been exemplary, to say the least — I was drowning in debt, and the apartment was a disaster. And then there was the old man: I felt guilty when I didn't visit, but while I was in the hospital, all I could think about were the things that were falling apart in the rest of my life. "Time," I said, "I need more time."

Ms Cornwall smiled. "Our most finite commodity."

"So that's what you're selling?"

"Not exactly," she said. "But Weltgeist can help you with both time and money. And you would be helping us a great deal, as well."

I was beginning to think I should have just sold the kidney. "How?" I said.

"For decades now, Japanese industrialists — who, like you and so many others, feel the conflicting pressures of family obligations and work — have employed actors to play the roles they are unable or unwilling to play in their own lives: an actor to visit aging relatives, attend family gatherings. One actor even made a living pretending to be a husband and father to several different women."

"So you want me to hire an actor to play me and visit my old man?"

"Not exactly. Are you familiar with artificial intelligence?"

"I've seen *Terminator*: it doesn't end well for humanity." I pushed my chair back. "I'm sorry, but I already have enough insanity in my life." I stood up. "Thanks for the coffee," I said.

"Wait," she said. "Give me five more minutes."

I hesitated, thinking about the hole I was in. "Shit," I said. I sat back down.

"I represent a team of some of the most brilliant minds in several fields," she said. "Engineers from MIT, psychiatrists from Cornell and Berkeley, doctors from Harvard and Stanford."

"Impressive," I said. "But I can't afford to keep the old man in this place, let alone pay for a team of doctors from Harvard."

"As I said, you can provide invaluable assistance to our research. In return, Weltgeist is willing to pay for your father's care and treatment."

I was stunned. It seemed like a miracle was happening. Unfortunately, I didn't believe in miracles. "Let me see if I follow," I said. "You have a robot that looks like me visit with my old man while I carry on with the rest of my life—a doppelganger?"

"Technically, it's an artificially intelligent simulacrum, not a robot."

"Jesus, are you for real?"

"The acronym is, appropriately, 'TIME'—'Therapeutic Intuitive Mitigative Ersatz'.

"Sounds like a name science geeks would come up with."

"Nerds, not geeks."

"Sorry."

Over the next half hour, she outlined a potential arrangement: a simulacrum, TIME, would be programmed with personal information about me, my family, my father's life; it would made to resemble me in outward appearance, to move and sound like me, and to devote itself to taking care of the old man.

"The TIME unit is patient," Ms Cornwall said. "It won't become frustrated with your father's questions or behaviours. It can learn, adapt, intuit moods, and interpret facial expressions. All of its interactions with your father will be recorded, and you will be able to view them over a secure server. Any behavioural changes you would like to see can be programmed almost immediately."

"Can I think about it?" I knew I should cut and run, but I was drowning, and this was the only life preserver currently up for grabs.

"Call or text the number on the card," she said, "when you make your decision." She stood to leave. "AI is already an indispensable part of the modern world. It has the potential to free us from the mundane, to give us more time for the things that matter. It's only logical that AI should help us care for our loved ones."

"Maybe being human means bearing your own burdens sometimes," I said as the clicking of Ms Cornwall's heels faded away. I stuffed her card in the pocket of my shirt.

Traffic was light on the freeway for a change, and by the time I reached my exit, I had pretty much talked myself out of accepting Ms Cornwall's offer. Maybe there was more duty than love in it, but, whatever else he was, he was my old man. Why should anyone else take responsibility for him?

It wasn't until I got back to the apartment that I realized that I had forgotten to hit a drive-through — score another point for Father of the Year. I checked Finch's room: he was asleep, or at least pretending to be. "Love you, son," I said. He mumbled something and rolled over. "Good talk, son. See you in the morning."

Judging from the state of the kitchen, Finch had made dinner for himself: the shrapnel scattered across the countertop suggested nachos. The kid was gonna get scurvy if he didn't watch out. I washed the dishes and wiped everything down. Maybe a robot wouldn't be so bad after all, I thought.

I dragged out my briefcase, momentarily plagued by guilt at not having graded the term papers that were fossilizing inside. I closed my eyes, and the feeling passed. I poured three fingers of Glenfiddich instead, put the briefcase back by the door, and sat down to check my email: two ads for Viagra, one from a Nigerian princess in distress, and one tantalizing penis-enlargement offer. I deleted them all.

The next message made my heart sink. It was from my ex-wife's lawyer, telling me I was behind in my alimony payments, blah, blah, blah. Great, just what I needed. I deleted that message, too.

The ex had shacked up with a cop, an alpha-male barbarian with a shaved head, and far more muscles than brains. He was nearly twice my size, so even in my revenge fantasies I ended up getting my ass kicked. She'd never marry him, though — not until she had bled me dry.

When she moved out, she had taken Finch with her. That only lasted until the kid got caught at school with a bag of weed. Then she'd called up, begging me to take him: Sergeant Testosterone wouldn't stand for a stoner in the house, it wouldn't be good for his career. Boo hoo. I didn't give a damn about any of that. I was just glad to have Finch with me.

The last email was the worst. It was from the school. Finch was suspended for possession of marijuana and would not be allowed to return until I had met with the vice-principal. Christ. No wonder he ate so many nachos.

I drained the Scotch and texted Regan Cornwall. *I'm in. What next?*

Her reply came back immediately: *Great. You won't regret this! Meet tomorrow?*

How's 5?

Perfect. Text me your email address. I'll send over some documents.

I went to sleep that night thinking of Frankenstein.

I began the next day by getting into a fight with Finch. I tried my best to be patient, but I could tell I wasn't getting through. Finally I suggested that maybe we needed to get some professional help, find someone he could talk to.

"That's your solution for every problem," he said.

"What is?"

"Pass it off to someone else."

"I'm doing my best," I said. "You didn't come with an instruction manual."

"Whatever."

"I have to go to work," I said after a long silence. "We'll talk about this later."

"Whatever."

I drove to work feeling sick, my knuckles white on the steering wheel. I mumbled my way through a lecture on the role of the Fool in *King Lear*, got an earful from Ms Webb, Finch's vice-principal, and scheduled an appointment to see her later that week. I texted Finch, but he didn't reply. I began to get that drowning feeling again. Since no students had scheduled appointments to see me during office hours, I needed something to take my mind off of my subpar parenting skills: I opened the email attachments from Regan Cornwall. They wanted a lot of personal details, pictures, videos, recordings of my voice.

Ms Cornwall was waiting for me in the cafeteria when I arrived at the hospital. She waved me over. "Matt," she said. "Glad you could make it. I need you to sign some documents. Please, take your time and read them over." She handed me the papers and a thick, black pen. I read and signed. In the harsh light of the cafeteria, the ink looked a little like blood.

A week later, I met TIME. I was impressed. Outwardly, it looked like me: same hair, same eyes, same features, same clothes. From thirty feet away, anyone would be fooled; close up, you could tell it wasn't quite human. The skin didn't look right for one thing, and there was something about the way it moved that wasn't altogether natural. The eyes were the right shape and colour, but they drew you down into them, leaving you searching their depths for something that could not be found. "Pleased to meet you," I said.

"I'm pleased to meet me, too," TIME said. It laughed, and it was like a parody of my own laughter.

"Are you ready for this?" Ms Cornwall said.

"What do I have to lose?" If I had thought about it a bit longer, I probably could have answered that question for myself.

Seated with a laptop in the lounge just down the hall from the old man's room, I watched through TIME's eyes as it pushed through the door to 1201A. The old man was over by the window, yelling at Rose. She looked up, smiled at not-me. Then I watched the smile fade. She made the sign of the cross and headed for the door.

The old man turned. "Wally?"

"I am dead," I heard TIME say. "I died in Vietnam. I stepped on a fragmentation grenade."

I clicked the chat box on the screen: "WTF?" I typed, along with the timestamp from the video. Immediately, another dialogue box popped open: "Sorry. Problem with the pronoun subroutine. Reprogramming now."

The screen flickered, and I heard TIME say, "Wally died. I'm sorry."

"Who the hell are you?" the old man said.

"Matt, your son."

The old man leaned in close, staring into the machine's eyes. "No, you're not," he said.

"I am going to stay with you," TIME said.

The old man walked over to the bed and sat down. TIME followed. "Go get Maria," the old man said.

The machine sat down beside him. "I'm sorry," he said. "Maria's dead."

The old man collapsed on the bed and began to moan, a low wail like a beast in pain. I watched as the machine reached out and took the old man's hand and held it.

I closed the laptop and went home.

Over the next few months, I visited the old man once or twice, but he was fading quickly. Rose continued to avoid the machine, defiantly crossing herself whenever they were in the room together. The old man was bedridden and frequently unconscious. Sometimes he woke up screaming, but he seemed incapable of speech. TIME was always at his side, holding his hand, dreaming its robot dreams as the old man slept.

At home, things were a bit better: I'd managed to get Finch

back into school, and he was talking to a counsellor — at Ms Webb's insistence, of course. I was even keeping up at work.

At night, I would log in and watch the recordings of TIME's interactions with the old man. There usually wasn't much to see, although I was surprised to see Finch walk in one afternoon. He must have taken my advice (for a change) and bussed down to the hospital after school. "Hello, Atticus," the machine said.

Finch stared right into its eyes. "I wish you were my real dad," he said. He kept staring for a long time before he broke into a smile. Little shit, I thought.

Finch stood over the old man. "Hey, G-dawg," he said.

"Your grandpa loves you," the machine said.

Finch looked up. "How the hell would you know?"

"I know everything about him," the machine said. "He wants you to remember him the way he used to be, not like this. He wants you to be strong."

Finch leaned over, put his arm around his grandfather's wrinkled neck, and whispered something in his ear. The old man murmured something I couldn't hear. "I love you, too," Finch said.

The end came a week later, just past midnight, according to the timestamp on the video. In the dim light, I saw the old man's eyes snap open, wide, terrified. "Matt?" he said.

"I'm right here," TIME said.

"I'm dying, Matt."

"It's okay to let go."

The old man's voice was hoarse, fading. "Something I got to tell you," he said. There was a long silence before he spoke again, "You always were terrible at sports, you know, physical stuff. Always with your nose stuck in a book." The old man wheezed, almost a chuckle. "I never understood."

"I know," the machine said. "You were disappointed in me."

"No," the old man whispered. I had to lean close to the computer to make out the words. "That's what I gotta tell you: you always tried so damn hard … to make me proud … so much I should have told you." He was gasping for breath. "Now it's too late."

I watched a hand that was not my hand reach out and touch the old man's shoulder, "It's not too late," TIME said.

"I was always proud of you," the old man said, "So proud, I …"

I watched as my father sank into deep water for the last time.

"I love you, old man," I heard the machine say.

------------------------------ ✴ ------------------------------

"Precisely at noon Pacific on Wednesday, June 3."

"That's rather particular, isn't it???"

"Indeed. But barring the odd glitch, I would mark your calendar."

"Why so?"

"The **Surrey International Writers' Conference** begins registration right then. And it can sell out in the blink of an eye. It's one of the most comprehensive professional development conferences for writers of all genres–crime, romance, thrillers–in Canada. I wouldn't want you to be disappointed."

"Ah, well, then, touché."

Surrey International Writers' Conference

October 23-25, 2020
Masterclasses October 22, 2020

Registration opens:
12 PM (PACIFIC TIME),
WEDNESDAY, JUNE 3, 2020

https://www.siwc.ca/registration/

------------------------------ ✴ ------------------------------

THE RAVEN SHORT STORY CONTEST

THE RAVEN SHORT STORY CONTEST

Intelligent, playful, fascinating: the 2019 Raven contenders were as captivating as the mysterious raven itself. We would like to thank JJ Lee, this year's judge, for his keen eye and insight. He had this to say about the winner and runners-up:

First Place: Michael Donoghue for 'Life4Sale'

'Life4Sale' showed in its epistolary structure a great command of character voice. The world building and the weird factor are efficiently established without ever forgetting that character motive and conflict are what make a short story tick. It never bogs itself down in spec fic mechanics. I appreciated that it is the kind of story you may find on Black Mirror *or, if you're old enough, classic* Twilight Zone.

First Runner-Up: MFC Feeley for 'Dannemora Sewing Class'

'Dannemora Sewing Class', a very short short story, daringly makes a section and POV break in the middle — and it works. The focus is on a single interaction, and we discover through the POV switch that it has ramifications. The story demonstrates the writer's skill and ability to inhabit characters with realistic diction.

Second Runner-Up: Rob McInroy for 'Zoroman's Cave'

'Zoroman's Cave' is a throwback with its hyper-intelligent yet sinister narrator reminiscent of Lovecraft's high-pulp narrators. The volume of verbiage and

contortion of the narrator's thoughts can come across as quite dense — high falutin', even — yet it flowed. It made for a smooth read. For that I thought it should be recognized as a standout and a great nod to the classic weird story genre.

Published here are 'Life4Sale' by Michael Donoghue and 'Dannemora Sewing Class' by MFC Feeley. Thank you to all submitting authors for offering us your best and supporting Pulp Literature Press. Congratulations to the above authors and the other seven shortlisted entrants in the 2019 Raven Short Story Contest:

Robert Bose for 'The Last Wave'
Soramimi Hanarejima for 'Controlling the Means of Production'
Claire Lawrence for 'Life Supports'
Jonathan Sean Lyster for 'Dad's Ghost'
Hannah C Van Didden for 'The Pang'
KT Wagner for 'Wax Agatha'
Matthew Vickless for 'Understudy'

Michael Donoghue *mostly lives in his head but resides in Vancouver, Canada. Michael works in public health, where he spends much of his time preoccupied with hand washing.*

MFC Feeley *wrote a series of ten stories inspired by the Bill of Rights for* Ghost Parachute *and has published in* SmokeLong, Jellyfish Review, Brevity Blog, Liar's League, *and others. Feeley has been nominated for* Best Small Fictions, Best Micro-Fictions, *and the Pushcart Prize, and was an Amazon Breakthrough Novel Award quarter-finalist. More at MFC Feeley/ Facebook and on Twitter @FeeleyMfc.*

$\mathcal{L}$IFE4SALE

BY MICHAEL DONOGHUE

Hey, I'm responding to your Craigslist ad in the Life4Sale section:

> "White Male, 31, Good Job & Health. Original Owner. Look-
> ing for Fast Trade.
> Post id: dHdpdHRlci5jb20vbXBkb25vZ2hlZQ==
> Male, avg looking, good health (one bad knee), awesome
> job, 31, no diseases, smoke-free, no pets or children. Look-
> ing to straight-up LifeSwap™ for equivalent trade-in due
> to recent divorce. Original owner, never swapped before.
> My loss — your gain."

Is it still available?

Maya

--

Hi,

Still avail, but not interested in selling to a woman, thanks.

--

Hi again,

Ha! Totally understand that feeling, but just to let you know, my original life body was male. Also, I've mostly traded and run male bodies, so no probs providing continuity for your aux life (friends/family/work/colleagues, etc.) Btw, what is your awesome job?

I'm looking for a straightforward LifeSwap.

Female, 27, mixed race (sold to me as being Japanese/Norwegian, but I have my doubts), curvy, moderate eczema, some Crohn's disease, steady employment in a flower shop (4 days a week). Comes with two pet rats and large extended family, plus a hot girlfriend (yes, you read that right). Am enclosing photo of g/f Cynthia.

Please let me know if you're interested.

Maya

--

Hi Maya,

Hadn't considered going female before, but wow. Any other girlfriend pics?

I'm a hotel inspector for Hyatt. So lots of free travel, food, and — of course — accommodation.

What state are you in? Me: Chicago. I'm looking for a new life somewhere very far from here, but unconcerned about the actual location.

B.

--

Hi B.,

I'm in Riverside, which is on the outskirts of LA. Nice and sunny all year around. Not sure about Chicago. I grew up next door to you, in Indiana, and remember how bitterly cold it can get if you don't dress for it. Weather is important to me. If you travel lots, can you move cities and keep your job? I'm really only considering Lifes in the southern part of the US or Hawaii. Does your Life come with any religious entanglements?

Am enclosing two more Cynthia pics.

Regards,
Maya

--

Hi Maya,

Here's a spreadsheet showing past four year's finances. Full disclosure: note the spousal support starting this year. Can you provide the same?

Chicago gets cold, but you're right. I learned young that if you dress for it, you hardly notice. Hyatt's HQ is here, so job location is fixed. But I share a rare window office on the 45th floor — terrific view.

Along with the standard Surface 1 memories of friends, family, and routine, I'd like to leave you with all 15 years, Levels 1-3, of my girlfriend/wife. Of course, you never have to access them; I just need to leave them all behind. I will include all Level 1 & most Level 2 memories for work (job quite easy) + will throw in a euphoric Level 3 memory of me winning the basketball state championship as an incentive if you agree to take my wife memories. I'm just looking for a fresh start.

Send spreadsheets, a health report, and more g/f pics, please.

B.

--

Hi B.,

Nice, I'm a basketball fan myself. My original bio kids were big b-ball players. And your finances look good. Have enclosed mine, as requested, and a health report.

Do you get much time off with your job? Or do you wake up each morning in a near identical hotel room and struggle to remember what city you're in before rushing to your next flight to your next identical room? Do you get any time to explore the places you visit? How does it work?

Could you answer the religion question, please? I'm Wiccan right now, but more spiritual than religious. In a previous swap,

I unexpectedly ended up in a severe Evangelical setting. Not my thing. I grew up Presbyterian-lite. Also, can you enclose some older photos of you so I can see how you're aging?

Here's a video of Cynthia and me on holiday in Mexico.

All the best, Maya

--

Maya,

Sorry, missed the religious question.

Presbyterian too. Also lite, but I can throw in the Level 1 memories if needed. Haven't gone regularly since childhood.

Yeah, I grew up in Indiana as well, so I know the weather can be really tough on people. Nope, work trips don't allow time off in between visits, but I (you) have flexibility in the planning. It's possible to schedule all the southern inspection trips for the winter.

Would you be willing to include some Level 2 and 3 memories on Cynthia if we trade? Or does she already know you're planning to trade Lifes? She's a big attraction to your trade, so I wouldn't want to go with only Level 1 and have her figure out after a month or two.

Also, I noticed in your health report that you're left-handed. That's really an undisclosed impediment and significantly reduces your value/market. I'm offering a good package here. Even with the support payments, my income is 2.5 times your current income. I should let you know I'm considering several other Lifes but want out of this one ASAP, so time is the biggest factor. I feel sick all the time and just want the hurt to end. Can you commit to making a trade in the next 24 hours?

I have savings of $50,000 in an offshore account that I planned to access after the LifeSwap but am willing to offer you $15,000 of that as an incentive if we can complete within the next day.

As requested, here's some photos of me five and 11 years ago.

B.

--

Dear Brad,

I'm sorry things are hard for you right now since you and Ann broke up. (How many 31-year-old male basketball state champion Presbyterians from Indiana with names beginning with B can there be? But the old photos clinched it.) I know I really don't have the right to offer you advice since I skipped out on you and your brother 15 years ago, but please don't make the same mistake I did. LifeSwapping right after your mother divorced me was the biggest mistake of my contiguous life. I know now that I should have stuck around for you and your brother's sake. I regret that a lot. Since then, I've been constantly hopping from Life to Life, at least twice a year, and it hasn't brought me any of the peace of mind I wanted. In fact, it's been the opposite. LifeSwap isn't the answer. Not a day has passed when I haven't wondered about you and Allen. I know how attractive a swap seems at a time like this. Don't be fooled; don't believe the ads. It isn't a second chance. Wherever you go — even to a different city, with a different body, and with a different life — you're still the same person. What makes you happy now, what makes you sad, what you find funny—they always stay the same. No matter what age, sex, or race you become.

I understand if you don't want to hear from me again, but I'd welcome the chance to reconnect if you're open to that.

Your Dad (Maya).

--

Yo Maya,

what up?! so, i'm just trolling Old Brad's email and found this gem!!! wicked!! he didn't include this memory in our LifeSwap—duh—but looks like he forgot to empty his deleted emails folder. D'oh!!!! what a n00b! anyway, dunno what to tell u. he didn't offer me any of his savings for my trade, if that makes u feel any better. scumbag! U wuz a bit preachy tho. if u wuz my deadbeat dad, i wouldn't have replied either tbh! (hold on, roooooooooom service has arrived!!! Friggin A!!!!!!). the job is AWESOME but there is soooooo much shit from my boss. Old Brad never said how much of a stickler they is for Deee-tail! so this life not as good as he promised, that's 4sure. anyway, he's now a 18 years old kid in lebanon, texas. ummmmm, yeah, if u want to find him, i guess u could try my old gamer tag: n00b_killer69.

"Brad"

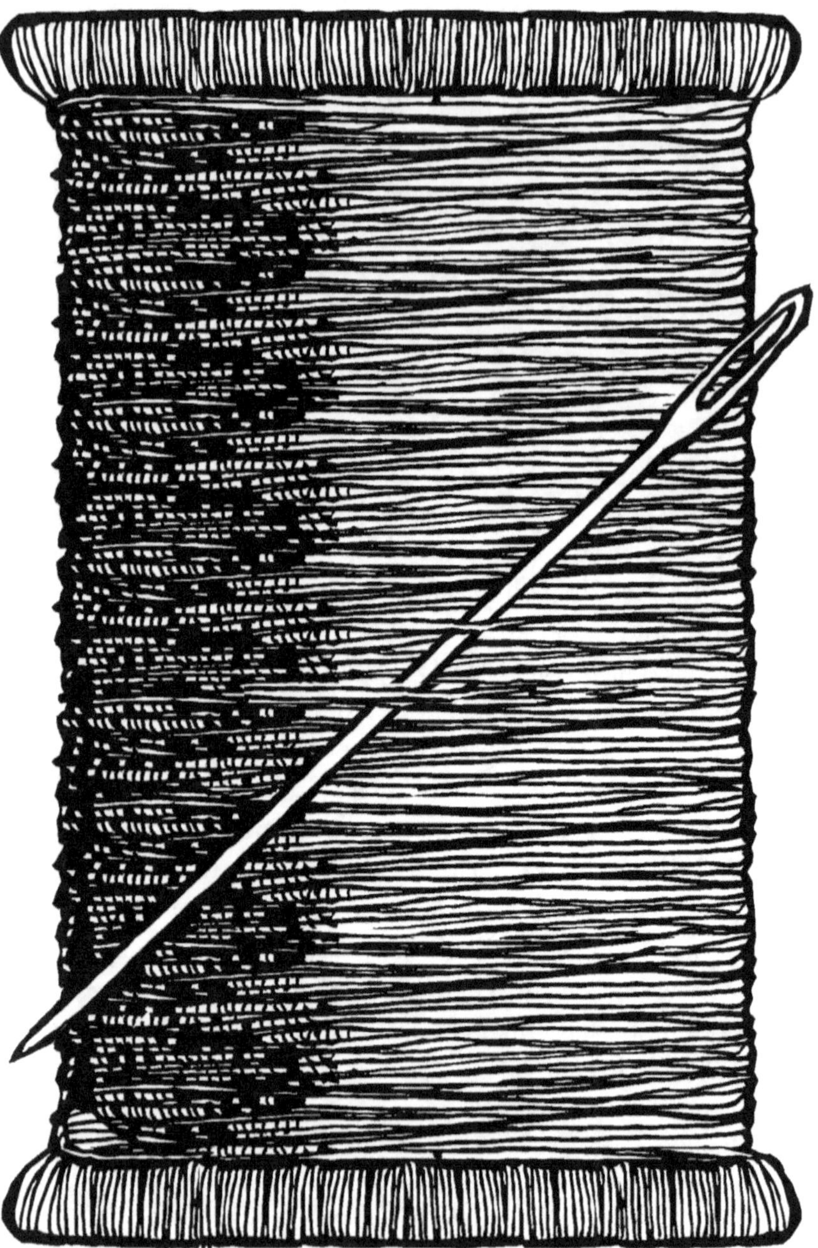

Dannemora Sewing Class

BY MFC Feeley

She leans across him to adjust the thread's tension, and he drives his nose into her armpit. His slow blooming smile doesn't alter his features but suffuses them with warmth. His eyes drop to breasts and bounce back; he mouths the word 'bobbin', lips bouncing on the *b*.

It's the first time he's spoken to her. Angie feels a tingle. His foot lifts off the pedal. Angie watches his hands, clean but discoloured from years of labour, pinch a wrinkle bunching under the presser foot and rub it away. He traces a circle where the wrinkle had been and prods the centre. Angie sucks in her breath. He resumes his seam, the faintest twitch tugging the right corner of his mouth.

Angie reminds herself what those hands have done, why he is in prison. As he smoothes the coming seam, she loosens the fabric stuck to her flesh where his nose drove in.

She brings her lips together in the *b* sound. Zippers are tricky. A zipper will keep him in line.

He inhales her, a warm mix of sweat and deodorant with a slap of Ivory soap. Is that ketchup? She eats her eggs with ketchup. A man with nothing but time, Ralph could stay there all day.

The weave of synthetic fibres and cotton imprint hatch marks on his nose. The seam beneath his fingers is hard like a two-lane road, but won't lie flat. Cars would topple off. Ralph pushes until the joining fabric gapes. Straining the thread.

He shuts his eyes. Does she shave, or does this sleeve hide a mass of curling hair? If he inhales hard enough to maybe unwind one, pull it through the coarse weave until it streams up his nostril and embeds with his own hairs, sticking to them, becoming his.

But that would be too much. He'd never get this close again, so he sucks exactly as hard as a preschooler pulling snot into his head so the teacher won't wipe his nose. (He'd like this teacher to wipe … but that will come.) He catches the teacher's eye and holds it. He'll wait a week to touch, maybe even to look, at her again. Next time on the wrist—

He can't think about that now.

Ralph likes sewing. Making roads. Bringing things together. French seams flat enough to skate on. Zippers like the thinnest blade of a hacksaw.

"Your zipper should never show," she says.

You know what else doesn't show? The little guy popping up from under the road, the bobbin holds everything together then, with one tug, unravels it all. He's the whole machine. He's the difference between a woman sewing alone and two threads weaving the future.

Ralph twitches his lip the way women like and mouths, 'bobbin'.

Angie stiffens. It's as good as a blush.

It takes nine months, but their zipper comes together, apart, together until their son, the slimmest echo of the male side of the zipper appears, the tiniest hacksaw on the market, loved and tucked safely in a perfect French seam.

PULP *Literature*

Four awards for genre-busting fiction and poetry

The Bumblebee Flash Fiction Contest

Deadline: 15 February
Prize: $300

The Magpie Award for Poetry

Deadline: 15 April
First Prize: $500

The Hummingbird Flash Fiction Prize

Deadline: 15 June
Prize: $300

The Raven Short Story Contest

Deadline: 15 October
Prize: $300

For more information visit: pulpliterature.com/contests

Short stories, poetry, and comics you can't put down.

DOUBLE FLUSH

Rina Piccolo

Rina Piccolo's *cartoons have appeared in numerous magazines including* The New Yorker, Barron's Business Magazine, Reader's Digest, Parade Magazine, *and more. Her co-authored daily comic* Rhymes With Orange *is syndicated in newspapers and websites worldwide. Her work appeared in* Pulp Literature *Issue 16 with the far-out tale 'The Vanishing Dot', and in Issue 7 with the skin-crawling illustrated story 'The Power of Centipedes'. Rina lives in Toronto, where she was born and raised.*

WHEN A DOUBLE FLUSH IS NECESSARY
by RINA PICCOLO

WELL, MY NEAR DEATH EXPERIENCES LEFT ME WITH ENHANCED SENSES FROM BEING IN CONTACT WITH THE AFTERLIFE.

I'VE BEEN BLESSED WITH THE ENERGY OF THE COSMIC LIGHT...
AND THE POWER HAS REMAINED WITH ME
...THERE WAS A MAN IN MY LIFE AT THE TIME, BUT...

HOLY SHIT, LISTEN TO THIS WOMAN! I CAN'T WAIT TO TELL EVERYBODY ABOUT THIS...
UGHH... CAN'T PEE!

...I CAN'T TELL YOU HOW, OR WHY IT HAPPENED TO ME, BUT BECAUSE OF MY ENLIGHTENED...
C'MON, PEE!
WHY CAN'T I PEE?

SHIT, IF I PEE NOW IT'LL SOUND DISRESPECTFUL TO HER NEAR DEATH EXPERIENCES...
MAYBE THE REASON I CAN'T PEE IS BECAUSE SHE'S DISTRACTING ME!

...AND MY BOYFRIEND AT THE TIME HAD A CHILD FROM AN....
FOCUS! PEE! PEE PEE!!

DRIP
PLIP
JESUS, THAT'S ALL?
ALL THAT EFFORT FOR TWO DROPS!?
...BECAUSE AS YOU KNOW AURAS CAN TRANSCEND THE PHYSICAL...
YEAH, I KNOW... IT'S ANOTHER REALM —I KNOW
IT'S IN THE SPIRIT REALM WHERE WE...
SHIT, NOW I HAVE TO FLUSH
I CAN'T INTERRUPT HER SPIRITUAL MESSAGE WITH A TOILET FLUSH ...IT'S THE ULTIMATE INSULT!
IT'S ONLY TWO DRIPLETS. MAYBE I'LL JUST LEAVE IT.
HOW SAVAGE OF ME...I CAN'T NOT FLUSH!
...AND THEN MY BOYFRIEND DUMPED ME...
THIS SEEMS LIKE AN APPROPRIATE POINT IN THE STORY...
...MY SPIRITUAL LOVE GROWTH AND

AFTER THE FLUSH SHE SAYS...
WHEN THE MAN WALKED IN HERE, HE HAD CALLED OUT, SO I DID HEAR HIS VOICE.
PARDON?
HE ANNOUNCED HIMSELF WHEN HE CAME IN. THAT'S HOW I KNEW IT WAS A MAN.
OH.
...BUT EVEN IF I DIDN'T HEAR HIS VOICE I STILL WOULD'VE KNOWN IT WAS A GUY BECAUSE OF MY ENHANCED INTUITION...
THE FLAVOUR OF HIS AURA WAS ENOUGH TO TELL ME.
AS YOU KNOW MALE AURAS ARE MORE AGGRESSIVE THAN FEMALE...
...MALE AURAS HAVE A AND MY SENSE CAN T
FLUSHHH
SOMETIMES A DOUBLE FLUSH IS NECESSARY.
NOW I GOTTA PEE.
Piccolo
END

THE SHEPHERDESS: PARIS

JM Landels

The second novelette in the La Bergère series finds shepherdess and budding entrepreneur Toinette on the left bank of the Seine, having just escaped four unsavoury gentlemen who offered her more than just a carriage ride to Paris. Toinette has lost her handcart and all but a single half-used pot of the lanolin cream she had been planning to sell in the city, but she has somehow gained a dog (Rafael), half a horse (Marteau), and a would-be saviour of questionable character (Henri).

__JM Landels__ is torn between travelling the world to teach writing and swordfighting, and never leaving her idyllic farm in Langley, BC. Her first book, fantasy bestseller Allaigna's Song: Overture, *is available from Pulp Literature Press and Amazon, and the sequel,* Aria, *is due out soon. You can follow her adventures with pen and sword at jmlandels.stiffbunnies.com.*

The Shepherdess: Paris

Even in the dingy, close front room of the inn on rue de la Harpe, the sounds and smells of the street pressed in from the open door and window. And this was still only the left bank. I could hardly imagine how crowded and noisome it would be once we were across the Pont Neuf. We had stopped to rest here because the place was too small to have a carriage yard in which Sauvegarde and his companions might easily pull up. Marteau was tethered in the alleyway, and I only hoped he would still be there when we emerged. The innkeep brought a board of cheese and bread. The former was waxy and curling at the edges, the latter dry, but at this point I was too ravenous to care.

"So mam'selle," said Henri between giant draughts of beer, "to what address now?"

In truth, I had none. My first destination was to have been the cart-hire, but since Claude, wherever he was, now had the cart, I had nothing to return. My intent had been to sell my pots of hand cream at the market on Île de la Cité, but I had none of those either. Just the one half-used jar of lavender.

I blinked to clear the heavy pipe smoke from my eyes and took a sip of beer to ease the rawness of my throat. I had a dog, half a horse, and, it seemed, a hanger-on of sorts — protector or parasite, I wasn't sure which. The latter felt closer to the truth when I was forced to empty the last few sols from my purse to pay for our dinner. All charade of knowledge and purpose dropped away.

"I confess, m'sieur," I said, "I am at a loss. Without my wares, I cannot hope to pay for rooms in the city for long."

He banged his cup down onto the table, making the cheese knife and Rafael jump. "Well, why did you not say so sooner, mam'selle? We have been riding all day in the wrong direction!"

The weight of desperation was a cold ball in my chest that would not let me speak. I put my face in my hands and willed tears away. A wet snout pushed its way between my wrists, and Rafael let out a whine that turned to a growl when Henri's large hand settled on my shoulder. The snout withdrew, but the growl continued.

"There, there, mam'selle." Henri lifted his hand. The growl stopped, and the nose returned. "I have many friends in this city whom we can depend upon for a bed for the night. And in the morning, that escu you have sewn into your cloak will buy you passage on a coach back to your St Geneviève."

I looked up. How did he know about the escu? "I never said where I was from."

He shrugged. "Oh, mam'selle, last night when I found you, you could only have come on foot from either Sainte Geneviève-des-bois or Viry-Châtillon. And there are no sheep farmers in Viry."

"What about sheep farmers?"

He took my hand in a paternal grasp. "My dear, fingers as soft as yours are found only on noble ladies and shepherdesses."

I snatched my hand away, too exhausted and miserable to pretend to be affronted. In fairness, I supposed very few ladies pushed handcarts.

"Finish your dinner, mam'selle," he advised. The last ferries run at dusk, and you can bet Sauvegarde's carriage will be stopped near Pont Neuf."

We had to ride another mile or so west to the horse ferry, and it was nearly dark by the time we got there. Marteau was reluctant to board the teeming, flat-decked boat, and I can't say I blamed him. It took Rafael nipping at his heels and a swat across the rump from Henri's scabbard before he launched himself forward, overturning another passenger's basket of plums and a cage of disgruntled ducks as he scrabbled to find footing on the overloaded planks. I sympathized with his wide eyes and splay-legged stance. I had never been on a boat before either. The Seine was much wider and deeper than the Orge back home, and the water splashed ominously over the deck. I envied Marteau and his four legs as passengers of all shapes and species shifted to find balance.

The far embankment was barely visible through the mist, and though the crossing seemed interminable, the lurch as we touched the jetty still came as a shock to me and to Marteau. He scrambled again, almost stepping on my toe, and knocked over another passenger as he charged off, Henri in tow.

This is where you wanted to be, I kept reminding myself.

With my bad ankle, I was the last to hobble off the deck. As I stepped onto the cobbled embankment, a lightness filled me. The air was different here. Warmer, with a slight odour of overfilled gutters to be sure, but alive with possibilities. I was injured, near penniless, and keeping company with dubious strangers in a city larger than any I'd ever been in before. And yet, I felt that I was home.

Henri left me sitting on Marteau's back outside the house on rue des Bons Enfans, as if he were unsure enough of his reception that it might be necessary to leave rapidly. It was full dark now, so only the thin moon and the orange light from the upstairs window illumined Henri's bulk as he knocked on the door.

A woman opened the ground-floor shutters. She was already in her nightcap, but that was all I could see of her. "What?"

"Hello, Mathilde," said Henri. "Will you open the gate for our horse, good woman?"

I could hear her scowl though I couldn't see it. "At this hour? I think not. Come back in the morning. Madame has retired for the night."

"Her lamp is still lit." Henri pointed to the window above his head. "And I didn't ask to see Catherine; only for you to let us in the yard. The laws of hospitality demand it, Mathilde."

The slamming of the shutters masked the details of the curse Mathilde uttered, but a few minutes later the tall wooden gate next door swung open. Henri took Marteau's bridle and led us into the stable yard, where he lifted me down from the saddle in an almost gentlemanly fashion.

"Mathilde," he said to the white-gowned figure, "This young lady has been thrown from a coach and dunked in a river. Be nice to her."

Mathilde sighed and motioned with her head. "Come," she said, opening a door into a dimly lit hall. "But not that creature," she said, shutting the door and leaving both Rafael and Henri in the yard.

As I limped behind Mathilde, who, I determined, must be a housekeeper rather than the lady of the house, I felt my insides relax for the first time in two days. My guts responded with a rumble of hunger that the sweaty cheese and stale bread had not quenched. My limbs went soft as well, and I had to support myself with the wall as I followed the woman. She paused between two doors and looked at me.

"Not the drawing room," she concluded, having raked me from head to toe with her eye. She led me into the kitchen. "Sit," she commanded, and my boneless knees happily complied.

She tossed some wood into the belly of the large iron stove and moved a kettle onto the centre of the hob. "So then," she said. "Who are you, why are you here, and why are you travelling with the likes of him?"

"My name is Toinette, madame. And Henri … he has been, uh, helping me. Since I sprained my ankle last night."

"Why?" she demanded.

"I fell in a ditch and twisted it when—oh." I realized she was asking why Henri was helping me. "Henri pushed my cart to the inn." Since that didn't quell the insistent frown on her forehead, I summarized the events of the previous night and this long day as best I could.

"You still have not said why he is helping you. Or why you are here."

I recalled then that the plan was for him to put me on a stagecoach home the next day, and I found all longing for the simple clean cottage and my village life vanished.

"He thought, Madame, that I might find work in your household." I picked up the corner of my cloak, ripped open the stitches, and pulled out the escu. "Though perhaps he is after this." I pushed it across the wooden table towards her. "Would your mistress take this as bond?"

Well, I had done it now, I thought. I had spent my last pistoles at the inn and given my escu to the housekeeper, who had taken it and given me a scrap of paper I couldn't read in exchange. But for the clothes on my back, the half-used pot of lavender cream, and the half a horse I hoped was stabled in the yard, I was penniless.

Mathilde led me upstairs. "There is no bed in the belowstairs made up," she declared, "and I shan't be going to that sort of trouble tonight. The guest room is free—you may sleep here for tonight. See that you don't make too much mess. You will clean it tomorrow."

I dropped an awkward curtsy. "My thanks go beyond words, madame."

She acknowledged my gratitude with the barest twitch of the corner of her mouth. Before she left the room she took an embroidered pillow from the brocade-covered armchair and tossed it on the bed. "Put that beneath your foot when you sleep." And then she was gone. I sat down on the bed and then fell over, partly in shock as my posterior sank into the padding. Feathers! Both in the coverlet and the mattress.

Yes, I thought, as I blew out the candle and sleep overcame me. Penniless I was, but tonight at least I would sleep like a duchess.

I was awoken by a knock on the door, followed immediately by the entrance of a girl no older than I. "Mathilde says you are to come downstairs at once." She held a folded white cloth in her arms. "She said you can borrow this until you make one of your own."

I guessed it was an apron like the one she wore.

"Merci, mademoiselle," I said, and moved to swing my legs out of bed.

I gasped at the stiffness in my back, my hips, and especially my thighs: a result of my several tumbles and my first ever day in a saddle.

As my feet touched the floor another, sharper pain shot up my right leg. My ankle, free of my boot, had swollen despite the pillow and looked like a mottled blue sheep's bladder.

I tried to stand and fell promptly back onto the plump soft-ness of the bed. "I'm afraid, mademoiselle," I said, "it may take me some time to comply. Could you bear the message that I will be down as soon as my sprained ankle allows it?"

The girl's eyes made an impressive tour of their sockets before she sighed and left the room.

I was tempted to lie back down and enjoy a last few minutes in the glorious bed, but I conceded it would not be the best way to begin a relationship with my employer, so instead I began gingerly pulling my stocking over my swollen foot.

That was hard enough to accomplish, but squeezing the foot back into my boot proved impossible. Blinking back tears of pain from the effort, I stood, tied the apron round my waist, and hobbled toward the stairs, one boot on, the other in my hand.

The stairs were a slow process, and I made my way down them leaning heavily on the handrail. As I reached the bottom, I could hear the rumble of Henri's voice. It was coming from one of the front rooms, and I edged towards it, wondering whether to seek him out or report to the kitchens as ordered. But I was late already—what difference would a few more minutes make? I lifted my head and decided to enter as the guest Henri had brought here rather than the domestic servant I was about to become.

I paused in the doorway, a handle on the frame for support, then backed out. I untied my apron and left it folded on the floor around the corner.

Once more I approached and, when poised in the doorway, gave a delicate cough, alerting Henri and the red-haired beauty who lounged opposite him, coffee cup in hand.

The hand that held that coffee cup was the whitest I'd ever seen. It was paler and smoother than that of Madame la Marquise or any of her coterie, with a blue vein that traversed it and continued up the inside of an even whiter arm that put to shame the fall of snowy lace at the elbow of her morning dress.

"Mademoiselle," said the beauty, putting down the porcelain cup and extending the hand toward me. "I am enchanted to make your acquaintance."

Though she did not rise or even sit straighter in the divan, a green-slippered foot shot out from beneath lace petticoats and struck Henri on the knee. This startled him into movement, and he put his cup down with a clatter, heaving his large frame out of the delicate furniture while I entered.

I took the woman's lily-white hand in my own sun-browned one and offered a provincial curtsy as Henri announced, "Catherine, this is Toinette. Haven't a clue to her surname, though Berger would be a good guess. Toinette, this is Madame Laferie, Marquise de Ruffiac and Countess of Athlone."

At that point in my life I had no idea whence either of the titles originated, but they were enough to deepen my curtsy. "Madame la Comptesse," I said, taking my hand from hers to spread my poor skirts as wide as they would stretch, in what I hoped was a suitably deferential posture.

Her laugh was like the tinkling of bells on a newborn lamb. "Please, Toinette, we do not stand on ceremony here," she said, waving that exquisite hand toward a silk-upholstered chair. "Will you take coffee? Henri, pour the girl a cup, will you?"

I sat, conscious of my travel-stained woollen skirt against the beautiful brocade, as incongruous as Henri's meaty fingers pinching the delicate handle of the cup as he poured black coffee from the ewer.

Coffee had never passed my lips before, and the strange aroma made my eyes water even before the hot liquid reached my tongue. I tried not to wince at the shocking bitterness, but the surprise must have shown in my face.

"Oh, Henri, you are a terrible manservant. Give the girl sugar."

Henri made an exaggerated bow to the Countess and with great show seized the silver sugar bowl. He pinched a brown crystal with the tiny silver tongs and held it above my cup. "Mademoiselle?" he asked with another overdone bow.

I winced again as a drop of hot coffee hit my wrist when the lump of sugar met the cup. Sugar was something I had had before, but only twice, and both times at the village epiphany feasts. I looked sadly at the cup and the sugar bowl, wishing the lump was in my mouth rather than wasted in the strong-tasting brew. It did make the coffee palatable, though.

"So Toinette," the Countess said, "Henri tells me you will be travelling back to St Geneviève-des-Bois today." She spoke with an accent I had not heard before. "You must give my regards to Edmonde," and here I realized she meant the Marquise.

It felt rude to interrupt, but I couldn't let her go on thinking I was a burgher's daughter. And yet it seemed even ruder to tell her I'd enlisted myself as a member of her household, especially as I drank her coffee as a guest.

I was saved the decision by Mathilde, who entered with a tray of brioches. "Oh, there you are," she declared. "You'd best make yourself more useful than this or you can take your bond and go home. *Vas-y!* There are chores waiting for you in the kitchen."

I put my cup down with a clumsy clatter and offered an even more clumsy curtsy. "I am delighted to meet you, madame." The words burbled out of me. "And I thank you for the coffee."

"Oh, take it with you." She waved that hand again. "You'll need it if Mathilde is putting you to work."

Her light laugh followed me as I left, nerves buzzing like houseflies as the few sips of coffee reached my veins. I glanced over my shoulder through the doorway and caught Henri's scowl. I gave a shrug and disappeared around the doorframe, scooping up the discarded apron as I limped to the kitchen.

I was elbow-deep in dishwater when Henri appeared at the kitchen door, the same scowl on his features. "You appear to have made a liar out of me, mam'selle."

I lifted an eyebrow. "I think that is a profession you are practised at, m'sieur."

He raised his massive shoulders then dropped them. "You have me there. But still, I feel there is much you have not told me."

"Sir, we have known each other but two days. There is bound to be much we have not told each other. For example, why you have followed me to Paris."

"Ah no, mam'selle, it is you who have followed me, I think."

I turned back to the dishwater.

There was a dramatic sigh. "Well, to be truthful, that escu in your cloak was an incentive." I looked back over my shoulder. "And a pretty face is hard to leave behind. Especially if I can deny Sauvegarde its pleasure."

"Ah. there," I said, "is one of those many things we have not told each other. What is your relation to those men?"

"That, mam'selle, is a tale for a longer time than I have. I promise I shall tell it to you someday. But now I have urgent business and bid you farewell." He bowed and prepared to leave.

"Not on my half of the horse, you don't."

He stopped, scowled again, opened his mouth as if to say something, and then turned and left the room.

Hobbling on my bad ankle and blistered feet, I was perhaps the slowest housemaid in Paris that day. Couple that with my utter unfamiliarity with the work, I was probably also the worst. It didn't help that, even though a housemaid was further up the social scale than a shepherdess, at least in terms of proximity to the high and mighty, I felt the work was beneath me. Mucking out a sheepfold seemed somehow more honest and dignified than cleaning up after a fellow human who had no cause to make such a catastrophe of the linens and chamber pot as Henri had. And, I admitted, it rankled to clean the room in which Henri had slept while he sauntered off to deal with his 'business'. I eyed the vase full of dried flowers, which sported a branch of cardoons, and resisted the temptation to nestle a few between the sheets. I had no idea, after all, if Henri would spend a second night here.

It took all morning to clean both his room and my own, twice the time it took Marie-Claire, the other girl, to do the mistress's room, that of the other gentleman guest—of whom I saw no trace of other than the linens Marie threw in the washtub—and the servant's quarters as well.

I felt my status sink lower and lower till I hobbled downstairs at noon, creeping at a tortoise's pace.

Mathilde was not unsympathetic. She made me put my foot on a stool while I ate my midday meal. Although it consisted mainly of leftover charcuterie from the mistress's dinner the previous night, I marvelled at the variety. At home we had mutton only in the autumn, and thin slices of *saucissons secs* the rest of the year. I felt a deep longing for a kitchen of my own full of exotic abundance, a furnished bedroom, and a staff to cook and clean.

Mathilde prodded my ankle, tsked, and wrapped it in strips of linen. "You should stay off it," she pronounced, lifting my spirits. "Marie-Claire," she said to the other maid, "bring buckets of water and the scrub brush." Marie's face darkened until Mathilde continued. "Toinette will do the floors."

Which did indeed take the weight off my ankle, since I spent the afternoon on my knees.

Henri returned in the late afternoon, by which time my knees, wrists, and back were as sore as my feet. He stepped over me as I worked on the last corner of the kitchen floor, his boots leaving flecks of manure from the streets.

"Are you sure you don't want to take that coach back home?" he asked, putting his dirty feet on the stool.

"I've no more coin," I said testily.

"Well, I will give you a ride back on Marteau — in exchange for the half of him."

I sat back on my heels, thinking. It was tempting. But where would I be? Back at home, like I was three days ago, but without savings or my pots of cream. Back below the bottom rung. No, I must be clever with what assets I had left.

"I thank you, but no, m'sieur. But I will sell my half of Marteau to you for three escus."

He snorted. "The whole of him's not worth more than four."

I stood my ground. I had spent time by the auctioneer's pens, and I knew a decent riding horse that was sound and willing could certainly fetch ten.

"And," I continued, "I will give you one back if you ride to St Geneviève to tell my mother I am safe, and get me some more lanolin."

By the end of the torturous first day, my situation at the house of the Countess seemed less like an opportunity and more like penance. But, I reminded myself, though I may be scrubbing floors today, I wouldn't for much longer. All I needed was some time alone with the Countess. And fresh supplies.

The latter was in progress with Henri's reluctant trip to St Geneviève, but the former was proving difficult. After my brief meeting with her in the morning, I did not spy so much as the hem of her skirts for the rest of the day. My sprained ankle kept me from serving the midday or evening meals — I was fit for scrubbing floors, dishes and laundry, but not fit to be seen. By the end of the second day, my knuckles were raw and the backs of my hands rough as a cat's tongue.

As I lit the stub of candle in the belowstairs room I was to share with Marie-Claire—no more feather bed for me—I reluctantly pulled out my last pot of cream.

It was more than half-empty now, the bottom of the clay jar just starting to show in the centre. I touched my finger to it and ran a miserly amount over the worst patches of my reddened hands.

Marie-Claire walked in, glaring with open resentment at my presence in her heretofore private chamber. I pretended to ignore her, focussing on my hands. What right did she have to complain? The room was twice the size of the cottage where I lived with Maman and my six siblings. And I had no doubt that if I wasn't cleaning the hearth and floorboards, it would have fallen to her. Surely she should be grateful?

She sniffed. "What's that smell?"

I looked up. Smell? Did she mean the lavender cream? "You mean this?" I asked, holding out the pot.

She took it, put her nose right into it. "Smells like mutton," she declared, handing it back.

I waved the pot under my own nose. Under the overpowering scent of lavender was the familiar smell of lanolin—an aroma so pervasive and common I discounted it. Granted, this pot had been open, and the lanolin would be faintly stale, but how could she tell under the lavender?

"You have a good nose," I said. "It is an older jar, and the lanolin is going off. Still, it's very nice on chapped skin. Would you like to try, mutton or no?"

She dipped a suspicious finger in the pot and brought out a dab large enough to make my heart sink.

"It goes a long way," I suggested. "That will do your feet as well."

She scowled again. "What need do my feet have of creams?"

A housemaid didn't get calluses from trudging over hills all day, I supposed. I shrugged. "The Marquise St Hilaire swore by it to keep her silk stockings from catching."

She snorted. "My stockings are wool."

I smiled. "Then your feet are already softer than a duchess's, since wool is what begets this. But," I added, "perhaps this smells better than stockings. Mutton and all."

She pulled off a stocking one-handed, rubbed the rest of the daub of cream into her foot, then put the hose back on. "We'll see," she challenged, "which foot is sweeter in the morning."

I put the lid back on the pot, afraid to look in and see how little was left. I folded myself between the sheets of my cot, missing the feather bed after only one luxurious night.

"Is there a flower market nearby?" I asked as she blew the candle out.

"What do you need flower markets for?" she retorted.

"The flowers in the drawing room—do they come from the garden, then?"

"Garden? What garden?" She snorted. "No, those are delivered every Friday."

If there was no garden, where did the herbs for cooking come from? I was about to ask that too, but was greeted by her snores.

Friday. Was that tomorrow or the day after? And when, if ever, would Henri be back? I fell asleep, planning.

I had thought Henri would have taken the dog with him, back to Claude perhaps. But when I carried the slops pail out through the kitchen door in the morning, there was Rafael, asleep on the step.

He jumped up and nearly toppled me, slops and all, thumping his tail against the doorframe and turning excited circles over my bare feet.

I cursed, shooing him back with the buckets I carried and hobbling to the midden. "Have you been fed?" I asked the giant grey animal, and then noticed from the well-chewed bones and the sizable deposits of turds about the yard that he had. I sighed, accepting that it was probably my job to clean those up as well.

The cobbled yard was shared by three other town homes in rows and contained a cistern, a dovecote, and stalls for four horses. A long-unused trap sat in one corner, covered in oilskin sheets. I drew a bucket of water from the cistern to wash down the cobbles, then left it half full for Jacques to have a drink. I was about to head back inside to face another day of scrubbing floors and fireplaces, when the bell by the kitchen door rang.

I jumped, and Rafael barked. "Sh!" I admonished him. "It's Henri, back from St Geneviève."

I hobbled across the yard to the gates and pulled on the chain that lifted the bolt. But when the door swung open, it was not the huge bulk of Marteau and Henri that filled the archway, but a small ass pulling a tiny cart full of flowers.

"Bonjour, mademoiselle," said the voice of the young man who was bent over the cart, retrieving an armful of chrysanthemums. "You're prompt this morning. Were you waiting for … Oh!" This exclamation was produced when he turned to face me and then said, rather stupidly, "You're not Marie-Claire!"

Rafael responded with a low growl from behind my knee. I put a hand on his head and was about to answer when Claire's voice came from the kitchen doorstep.

"Well spotted, Luc." She marched past me, took the armload of mums, and turned on her heels, heading back inside.

"On account again, mademoiselle?" called Luc.

"*Comme d'habitude*, Luc," she replied without looking back.

"But wait—" He had a note in one hand, no doubt the bill, and a spray of heather and tiny purple daisies in the other.

"I will take it in," I said, plucking the note from his hand.

"For Mathilde," he said.

I reached for the posy. "And is that for her or for Marie-Claire?" I asked.

"Today, mam'selle, it's for you." He took my hand and kissed it, chapped knuckles and all. I suddenly felt abashed for my travel-stained clothes.

Rafael growled again.

"Sh!" I hissed at him. "*Merci, m'sieur,*" I smiled, taking the posy and raising it to my nose. The daisies smelled horrible, but the heather would be useful. "Do you come here every week?" I asked, eyeing his cart.

"Each Friday, mam'selle."

"And how much for a spray of lavender?"

"Today, mam'selle, that will cost your name," he said, plucking a three-headed stem from the bunch.

"Toinette." I curtseyed, taking the precious branch. "*Merci,* Luc. À bientôt," I said as I closed the gates.

I tucked the lavender under the bib of my apron along with the heather, then rearranged the daisies into a respectable, if tiny, bouquet once more. As I passed Marie-Claire, who was stoking the kitchen fire, I dropped the daisies on the counter. "These are for you," I said as I continued on to our chamber to slip my floral treasures between folds of my spare clothes in the chest.

Mathilde I could not find anywhere, but I hobbled about the house searching rather than ask Claire. She worked the kitchen with a storm cloud over her head that I'd rather not disturb.

What story had I interrupted between her and Luc? I wondered. He was, I admitted, a handsome young man with striking dark hair and eyes. And was it not true my heart beat a little faster when he kissed my hand? It beat faster even now, just thinking of it.

But, I reminded myself, a flower seller was just a farmer in city clothes, and I didn't come all this way to go soft over a farmer when I could have had my choice of dirt-grubbers at home. He was useful, though, and I had two fresh flowers without spending a penny. Now if only Henri would return with the lanolin …

With these thoughts busying my mind as I searched for Mathilde, I scarcely noticed which door I was opening till I blundered into Madame's study.

She was still in her morning dress, quill in hand, making marks in a ledger.

"My pardon, madame," I stammered, backing out. "I was looking for Mathilde."

She looked up as if seeing me for the first time, and said, "Not at all, dear girl. Mathilde is at market this morning. Can I help you?"

"No, madame, I merely need to give her the bill from L—the flower seller."

"Well, you've saved a step, since she would give it straight to me anyway. She held out her hand, and I put the note into it, noticing the former was the whiter of the two. She read it, frowned, and stuffed it under the ink blotter. She leaned back in her chair and used her foot to push a stool out from under the desk.

"Paperwork is dreary," she said. "Sit. Tell me about yourself."

I said, "There is little to tell, madame. I am from a small village. Maman is a sheep herder."

"And Papa?" The question was almost sharp.

"I suppose he was too. But he died when I was young."

"So what is a young *bergère* hoping to do in Paris, then? We have no sheep here, as you might have noticed."

"The Marquise de Gentilly and her friends, they buy my pots of creams. I thought … I had hoped … there would be more customers here in the city." I looked down and smoothed my apron out over my knees. "But all my pots save one were lost when a carriage threw me in the ditch on my way here."

She cocked her head to one side. "How unfortunate. I am surprised you did not return home at once to re-supply."

I busied myself with my apron again. "I cannot go home, madame."

"Cannot, or will not?"

"Both, madame."

There was a tiny crease between her eyebrows as she looked at me with penetrating green eyes. I met them, pleading silently that she not ask me to elaborate. Instead, she said, "I too left home when I was very young."

What possible reason could a countess have to leave home? I wondered. Or was she just being kind?

"Were you married young, madame?" I enquired, since she seemed to invite enquiry.

She smiled. "Not as such. But this is your story, not mine. I do not see yet how your transformation from shepherd to would-be merchant to housemaid transpired."

So I told her of meeting Henri, the encounter with Sauvegarde and his crew. At the end she leaned forward. "It was not alto-gether wise to put your trust in Henri, my dear. Though given the alternative, you made the better choice. Henri's nature is questionable, but his heart is soft. The other four … are known to me. It was foolish to step into their carriage and dangerous to cross them. But what is done is done, and you are here now and safe." She reached out and took my hand. "You are welcome to stay in my household as long as Mathilde is happy with your work. I wish your hand creams had not been lost, though. I know the Marquise, and if she liked them, they must have been fine indeed."

I was tempted to hand over my remaining one, but Marie-Claire's assessment of it made me hesitate. It would be best to start with fresh lanolin. If only Henri would return.

At that moment, Marie-Claire appeared at the study door, giving me a cold look as I jumped to my feet.

"Madame," she said, dropping a ghost of a curtsy. "There is a gentleman to see you." She handed the countess a slip of paper.

Madame frowned as she read it. "Show him in," she said to Marie-Claire, and "Stay here," she said to me as she adjusted her hair and robe. "This is far too great a coincidence." The last was to herself, but it piqued my curiosity.

There was no exit from the study except through the drawing room, so as she left, I followed her to the open door and stood behind it, looking through the gap left by the hinges.

"M'sieur," she said. "To what do I owe this unexpected pleasure?"

I smelled his stale perfume before I heard his voice or saw his wig come into view. "Surely you must have visitors who come for the sole purpose of enlivening their day with the sight of your face, madame?" said Sauvegarde.

"Perhaps," she allowed, "but they usually give more notice." She sat, and motioned him to do the same.

"You have me there, madame. But this is a matter of some urgency, for I believe you hold something of mine. My niece."

"Your niece? I had no idea you had any."

"You would never have met my dear sister—she lives in a village not far from here. Her daughter was seduced by that rogue Dupin, who has brought her here under false pretences. You may have heard pretty tales of adventure, but I assure you my sister is distraught with thoughts of what that villain may have done with her. Let me return her to her mother, and we shall leave you blameless—as you no doubt are—in all this."

Behind the door, I was transfixed by threat. Would the *comptesse* believe him? Would I, were I in her delicate slippers?

The blood rushing in my ears made hearing her reply difficult.

"I believe you are mistaken, my dear Philippe. There is no niece of yours here."

I let out the breath I didn't know I'd been holding.

She continued. "Perhaps Henri took her someplace else?"

Sauvegarde's courtesy fell a few steps lower. He strode towards the window, and I could hear the twin bangs as he threw open both shutters. "Louis-Auguste," he called, then stepped back into my field of view again. "Do not play such games with me, madame. I beg you, come look out the window."

I longed and feared to see what was there.

"Now," came his voice, "if you'll be so kind as to direct me to my niece, we'll release this brigand to you to do with as you will."

"Would that I could, m'sieur," came her icy voice. "The girl you have mistaken for your niece left by coach for her home yesterday morning. Now release him, and be on your way."

"In that case, I have no use for him. Louis-Auguste," he called, his voice small, as if his head were out the window. "You may cut his throat."

Accompanying these words came the sound I now knew as steel being drawn from a scabbard. Fearful for the countess's life, I rushed from behind the door, shouting *"Non! I am here!"* I froze again at the tableau before me. Instead of Sauvegarde with his rapier in hand, it was the Countess who held the blade, its point levelled at Sauvegarde's chest.

My distraction, however, allowed him to slip his body past the point of the sword and grasp the weapon's intricate guard, wresting it from Madame's hand.

She yelped and jabbed her other elbow at his face, but she missed and stumbled forward as he stepped back.

I knew nothing of fighting, but I knew that you could topple the most truculent ewe if you could get a leg or two in the air. I rushed forward and threw my weight onto the end of the divan, slamming it into the side of Sauvegarde's leg with all my force.

It didn't topple him, but it did set him off balance long enough for Madame to wrap her arm around the blade of the sword and reclaim it with a swift jerk and a kick to the shin, which finished the job of unbalancing him. Sadly, he fell not on the floor but on the soft upholstery of the divan. She placed the tip of the rapier at the base of his skull.

"Do not move, sirrah. Louis-Auguste," she shouted in a voice more suited to a cow caller than a countess. Bring m'sieur Dupin to my door unharmed, and I will not skewer Philippe." She continued in softer tones. "I do hope, for your sake, that Louis-Auguste has some small care for your skin, Philippe."

She motioned with her head to the window. I needed no prompting to look out carefully, hiding my face behind the shutter. There stood the mountainous Henri in front of the carriage, his hands behind his back, a rag stuffed into his mouth, and sporting black eyes and a nose swollen even larger than drink had already made it.

"No, madame," Louis-Auguste called back. "Send Sauvegarde out the door unharmed, and I won't gut your friend."

The gaunt man stood casually beside Henri, on hand behind the large man's back, the other holding a long, slim dagger that rested below Henri's ribs, making a visible dent in the stained white shirt and flesh beneath it.

"Meet us on the stair," she called back.

In the window of the carriage I could see the twin barrels of Étienne's pistols and the wisps of smoke from their matches. Sanglier was doubtless around somewhere.

"Madame," I whispered, "there are two more of them in the carriage, with primed pistols."

"I know that," she said grimly. "Take the curtain tie." "She motioned with her left hand to the tasselled rope that held back the floral curtains.

I twisted it from its hook and brought it to her.

"Hands behind your back, Philippe," she said, pricking him in the neck with the sword.

He complied gingerly, and I wound his wrists with the cord, grateful for the shearing knots I knew. When the knots were as secure as I could make them, I stood back.

"On your feet."

He rolled over, looking daggers at her, his wig askew. With the tip of his sword, she flicked the wig off his head, exposing the grey stubble beneath.

"*Allons-y*," she said.

Sauvegarde stumbled ahead of us, the wickedly sharp tip of his own rapier resting on the back seam of his coat, just between the shoulders. It seemed to me that Madame held that ornate grip with more than a passing familiarity, but what did I know of swordsmanship?

"Open it," she said to me as we approached the front door, "but stand behind it. She shifted the tip of the rapier a hand-breadth to the left and turned her palm upwards, as if holding a platter of pastries, not a deadly piece of steel. She extended her arm slightly, and the point of the sword pressed into the fabric of Sauvegarde's coat.

"If your friend harms another hair of Henri's head," she murmured to her captive, we will find out if you have a heart to pierce, or whether you will die a slow, bubbling death from a bleeding lung." She said it with a smile, and a lilt to the voice, as if she were discussing the possibility of rain on the morrow or the price of barley at the exchange. Which didn't stop the beads of sweat from trickling down Sauvegarde's exposed neck.

I unshot the bolt, trying not to let my hand shake, and drew the door open, flattening myself between the heavy beechwood and the wall behind me. The countess gave a minimal prod, and Sauvegarde stumbled forward, steadying himself against the doorframe as he caught his spurs on the step. The tip of the rapier was now invisible, having pierced the fabric of his coat. I wondered if it had broached his skin as well.

"Gentlemen," called Madame, "do come inside. The day is warm."

I was puzzled at the invitation before I saw, through the crack between door and frame, the hats and cloaks of passersby. I also heard the creak of an ox cart on the cobbled street. A charade for the benefit of the neighbours, then.

"I'm afraid we must decline, madame," replied Louis-Auguste. "The day is waxing, and my friends and I have leagues to travel."

Madame gave a little twist of her wrist, and now I knew the rapier had touched flesh, for Sauvegarde yelped.

"Perhaps, Louis," he grunted through clenched teeth, "you and M'sieur Dupin should come in for a brief moment at least."

This could go on all afternoon, I thought, Louis-Auguste with his knife on Henri's back, Madame with Sauvegarde's rapier in his.

"Pardon," I said, and slipped out from behind the door and under Sauvegarde's hand.

I was still aware of the smouldering matches on Étienne's pistols from within the carriage, and so my trajectory down the steps kept Henri and Louis-Auguste between me and them. My blood was rushing through my ears so fiercely I could hardly hear myself think. Which was just as well, or I would have talked myself out of it.

I limped toward the pair of men, a smile on my lips, though perhaps not in my eyes. As I came closer, I curtsied. "Messieurs," I said as brightly as I could. "My mistress does insist." I came a step closer, my voice dropping so only they could hear. "It is all well and good, you holding your darling little knife to Henri's back, but if you compare it to his girth, I'm not sure it will reach any vitals. Now, M'sieur Sauvegarde's sword, on the other hand, is only about six inches away from his heart, and I believe Madame is quite serious in her intent to run it through to the hilt if you so much as prick Monsieur Dupin's hide."

I walked around to the other side of Henri, away from Louis-Auguste, so I could see the larger man's hand. It put me in line with Étienne's pistols, and the hairs on my neck tried crawling to my scalp, but I held my ground. "Now," I continued, "I will raise my hand and hold five fingers in the air. As I put one down, Madame will push that sword one inch into your friend's back. Two fingers, two inches, and so on. Unless you cut the rope on Monsieur Dupin's wrists and allow him to walk into the house."

As I said this, I began stepping back towards the house, circling to put bodies between me and Étienne again. "Henri, tell me when you are free." I held up my hand, fingers splayed, and started to curl the thumb slowly inwards.

There was a grunt from Henri, but at the same time, I was struck in the back of the knee.

It was Sauvegarde, who had tumbled forward down the stairs, away from Madame and into my legs.

I collapsed onto him as I watched Henri spring and elbow Louis-Auguste in the chin. A shot rang out, and I was sprayed in the face by stone dust as the ball cracked one of the steps. The second shot came a split second later, and made only the sickening sound of impact into flesh. And then a bone-jarring thud as Henri fell on both me and Sauvegarde. I felt the wind of skirts as Madame rushed past my face, then nothing more as breathing became impossible.

The world became light again as the weight was removed. For a moment I thought I was face down on the flagged floor of the shearing shed, but no, the dung between the stones smelled of horses, not sheep, and worse things as well.

I heard the scramble of eight hooves and the rattle of wheels amid shouts and the slamming of doors.

"Are you hurt, my dear?" Madame was crouching beside me, her perfumed skirts blocking the sight and scents of the street.

I came to one elbow, put a hand to my chin, and winced as my fingers touched raw flesh. "Not to speak of, madame," I lied.

As she helped me up, I realized my knees were bruised as well, and it felt like I'd cracked a rib to add to my still-recovering ankle.

"Dammit, Cat, I'm the one who's been shot!" grumbled Henri from behind me.

She looked over her shoulder at the large man, who was back on his feet, a meaty hand clutched to his side. "I can only help one person at a time, Henri, and you are already standing. Marie-Claire!" she bellowed in that farmer's voice, before dropping it again. "Where is the damned girl?"

Madame had hobbled me up the stairs and through the doorway by the time Claire appeared, suds dripping from her hands and her shirtsleeves rolled past the elbow.

"Where have you been, girl?" snapped Madame.

If Claire was in the middle of washing pots, she would have heard nothing over the clatter of casseroles and her own singing. Her face was a mask of confusion. She looked in horror at the blood dripping off my chin.

"Go on," said Madame. "Take her back to the kitchen. I'll look after this brute."

Madame handed my elbow to Claire, but I straightened, took hold of the wall instead, and made my own limping way to the kitchen in Marie-Claire's wake. I sat on the bench with a painful thud—apparently I had bruised my hip as well—and leaned my head in my hands, fighting off nausea.

"Don't drip on the table," snapped Claire, tossing a dishrag my way.

My chin was bleeding freely now, and indeed there were several dots of blood on the table. I wiped them with the rag as Claire slid a pan of water under my face. I dipped the rag in the water and began dabbing at my chin, slightly shocked at the swirls of red appearing in the pan.

"Let me see," said Claire. I lifted my head, and she winced.

"That bad?" I asked.

She handed me a clean copper pot from the rack overhead. In the swirly orange reflection, my face didn't in fact look as bad as it felt. A small split—less than a finger width—on the point of my chin was the source of all the blood. A scrape along my jawbone was the source of the pain.

I pressed the rag onto my chin to staunch further blood.

"Head wounds bleed a lot," I muttered through closed teeth. "It's not actually that bad." I thought of the numerous cuts, bruises, and scrapes my siblings and I had endured from hooves, horns, and errant shears, never mind our tumbles on the rough country terrain.

At that moment, Henri and Madame came in. She sat him next to me at the table and began helping him out of his coat, a process that engendered much cursing before the even more stained garment was removed. The shirt beneath was soaked red, and I shifted down the bench, not wanting any more blood on my very limited wardrobe.

Claire turned away and leaned on the sink. I wondered if she was going to vomit. Blood didn't bother me, but the increasing queasiness I felt from the pain in my ribs wasn't helped by the thought she might spew her guts.

Instead I glanced at Henri, who was now losing his shirt at the hands of Madame. "Hold still." She returned his curses with an equally salty tongue. "You're not dying, for your mouth is still moving."

With his shirt off, he seemed larger than ever, a mountain of dark flesh with a bright red streak along the line where ribs would be if they were not hidden by his girth.

"You are a lucky man," said the Countess, probing the wound with a kitchen knife and a look of distaste. "The ball went past you, just taking a furrow with it. If you were slimmer, it would have missed entirely."

"Woman, if I were slimmer, it would have hit my sword arm or my kidney. My fat has saved my life."

"It should still be stitched, or you'll bleed all over my house. Claire, when will Mathilde be back?"

Claire answered, looking at the ceiling, the stove, anything but Henri, me, or the blood. "Not till tonight, madame."

Madame cursed. "I'm not nearly as good with a needle as she … Would you stitch it, Claire?"

Claire's face drained white. "I … I … don't think I can, Madame." She bolted for the back door.

"I can do it," I said through the rag on my chin. "I've stitched up enough wethers at castrating time."

It was satisfying to see Henri's dark skin lighten a few shades as well.

I can't say my stitches were tidy. I am no seamstress, and Claire would have done a better job with her neat hand if she were not so squeamish. I wondered how she coped with monthly laundry with so many women in the house.

Henri took large swigs of brandy between each stitch and chewed on a balled-up towel when I stuck the needle into his hide.

"Henri," I asked as I paused to rethread my needle. "Why did Sauvegarde come here with an elaborate story about me being his niece?" I looked at him through the eye of the needle.

"Ah, well." He cleared his throat. "I believe he was not looking so much for you as for this." He leaned backwards on the bench, wincing as the stitches in his side stretched and a fresh trickle of blood ran down the roll of flesh above his belt. He undid that belt—causing me to raise my eyebrows in alarm—and began unwinding a long thread that wrapped the leather just behind the buckle. As the thread fell away, metal appeared, and he pulled out what looked like a dinner knife.

"He may believe you had this."

I picked it up. It was not a knife, but a letter opener, fashioned to look like a small, hiltless sword with an ornate gilded handle. I held it in one hand, my needle in the other.

"And why would he think that?"

Henri took another swig of brandy. "Ah, mademoiselle, that is a long tale, and I, ah, continue to bleed." He looked down. "Would you be so kind as to continue before I give you my theories?"

When I and the bottle of brandy were finished, I put down the needle and picked up the stiletto.

He shook the empty bottle. "I seem to be dry, mademoiselle. Would you?"

"Answers first," I replied, turning the letter-opener over in my hand, letting it come to rest with the point casually regarding his freshly sewn flesh.

"He seems quite fond of it," Henri said. "I took it from him at the inn. He seems to think *you* took it when you accepted the jaunty little carriage ride.

I stared at Henri, wondering how much help Sauvegarde had had coming to that conclusion. "And he's so fond of it, he's willing to hold you hostage, shoot you, and kidnap me to get it back?"

Henri shrugged. "Look at the insignia."

I peered at the ornate handle. In the flat spot where the thumb would rest was a graven sun with a flowery initial inside. My aunt had taught me letters, but none as extravagant as the engraved 'L'.

"*Le Roi?*" I asked.

Henri nodded. "Now why do you think a down-and-out pretender like Philippe Sauvegarde would have a pretty piece of cutlery belonging to the king?"

"I don't know."

"Neither do I," he returned, "but I aim to find out."

"Find out what?" came Madame's voice from the doorway.

Henri's reached out far faster and more casually than anyone as drunk as he should have been able, and before I could react, he'd reclaimed the knife and tucked it back under his vast girth. "What that rascal Sauvegarde wants with our fair shepherdess here," he said loudly.

I twisted on the bench to look at her. Her arms were crossed and her eyes narrowed. "Try another one, Henri. I'm sure whatever the reason, the fault lies with you. And whatever the reason, he's now left both her and this behind." She held up Sauvegarde's rapier. "I don't intend to be here when he returns. Go and put on a clean shirt, and when Mathilde gets back, we will move the household." She took two swift steps across the kitchen and placed her delicate white fingers under my chin.

"I am sorry about this, my dear. But it will be a small blemish, one that adds character and does not detract from your face."

The blood on my chin had dried, but I could feel the bruise growing as my concentration returned to myself.

"I hate to ask more of you," she continued, "but could you clean the kitchen before you change? Claire is hopeless around blood."

"Certainly, madame," I said as I raised my shaking, aching body to its feet. "But I'm afraid I have no clean blouse." My other one was hanging wet on the laundry line in the yard.

"Not to worry—I will lend you a change of attire. Claire will lay out fresh clothes. That at least she can do."

When the kitchen was clean and the last buckets of bloody water washed down the drain, I hobbled down to the room Claire and I shared.

She had changed already into a finer dress than I'd ever seen on a housemaid's back. To my shock, the one laid out on my cot was at least as fine.

Her face was still pale, but she had recovered her sharpness. "Hurry and change," she said. "I'll need to help you with the stays. The carriage will be here soon."

"Where are we going?" I asked, eyeing the arrangement of whalebone and laces with trepidation.

She looked at me as if I were the stupid one. "Versailles, of course."

THE ARTISTS

Tais Teng

Cover artist, Queen of Swords

Queen of Swords is the fifth cover painting by Tais Teng for *Pulp Literature*, and it is part of his Plucky Girls and Fearsome Ladies series. She is in the company of Grand-Admiral Isabella and the Hanged Queen of Lizards. Teng's previous pieces for *Pulp Literature* include *Youth Hostels of the Faery* (Summer 2014), *Pesky Summer Jobs* (Spring 2015), *Dieselpunk Explorers* (Winter 2016), and *After the Tsunami* (Summer 2018). The Dutch artist has also written a hundred books for both adults and children. Readers of *Pulp Literature* will recall his story 'Growing up with your Dead Sister' in Issue 8. You can find more of his art at deviantart.com/taisteng/gallery and you can read more about him on his website, taisteng.atspace.com.

Rina Piccolo

Artist, 'Double Flush'

Rina Piccolo's cartoons have appeared in numerous magazines including *The New Yorker, Barron's Business Magazine, Reader's Digest, Parade Magazine*, and more. Rina's work for *Pulp Literature* includes 'The Power of Centipedes' (Summer 2015) and 'The Vanishing Dot' (Autumn 2017). Her co-authored daily comic *Rhymes With Orange* is syndicated in newspapers and websites worldwide. Her syndicated daily comic strip *Tina's Groove* ran from 2002 to 2017.

Currently Rina's cartoons can be seen from Monday to Saturday in the comic feature *Rhymes With Orange* (King Features Syndicate). Rina is also the co-author of the book *Quirky Quarks: A Cartoon Guide to the Fascinating Realm of Physics* (Springer, 2016). She lives in Toronto, where she was born and raised. You can find more from Rina at rinapiccolo.com.

Mel Anastasiou
In-house illustrator

Mel Anastasiou loves drawing for *Pulp Literature* because she loves the stories she illustrates. She draws in black and white, working from imagination and inspired by details from Renaissance compositions. You can find more illustrations, as well as writing tips and news about her books and novellas, at melanastasiou.wordpress.com, and see her artwork on Facebook at Bird and Branch Artwork.

HALL OF FAME

These are the heroes — the Patrons and Pulp Literati whose monthly support helped bring you this issue. Please lift your glasses and give them a rousing cheer!

The Shareholders
Rapscallion

The Landlords
A Bursewicz
Isabel Cushey

The Innkeepers
Ada Maria Soto
Margot Landels
Ev Bishop
Shannon Saunders
Roger & Anne Anastasiou
Kevin Harris
Richard Ohnemus
Robin McGillveray
Sarah Farr
Gillian Gardiner

The Cicerones
Susan Lefeaux
Elsa M Carruthers

The Bartenders
Alana Krider
Richard Gropp
Ron Graves

Kristen Mah
Michelle Balfour
Robert Bose
Victoria McAuley
Dave Wayne
Scott F Gray
Abigail Bruce
Patrick Bollivar
Dietra Malik
Elaine McDivitt
Joshua Pantalleresco
Emily Lonie
Anna Belkine
Shannon Sinn
Katriona Greenmoor
Famille Bussières
RS Morgan
AD Bane
Multiverse Jumper
KT Wagner
Michael Weckworth
Danny Palacios
Terry Fries
Sarah Pendergraft
Deepthi Atukorala
Margot Spronk
Margaret Elliott

Iain Burns
Leny Wagner

The Regulars
CC Humphreys
Marta Salek
Rina Piccolo
Jenny Blackford
Jain Cairns
Michael Barrie
Leo X Robertson
Kristene Perron
Akemi Art
Peter Halasz
Kristan Cannon
BC
JW Horton
Walter
Miriam Zibkoff
Meredith Frazier
Heather Ane Wilkey
James Rumpel
Catherine Levinson

The Clientele
Ray Hsu
Melissa Hudson

If you would like to join the ranks of these worthies, you can become a patron on Patreon at patreon.com/pulplit, or join the Pulp Literati through our website at pulpliterature.com/join-pulp-literati/.

MARKETPLACE

$\mathcal{B}$OOKS

Advent *by Michael Kamakana* • We thought we knew what the aliens wanted. Think again. • pulpliterature.com/advent

Allaigna's Song: Aria *by JM Landels* • The long-awaited sequel to the best-selling *Allaigna's Song: Overture.* • pulpliterature.com/allaignas-song

The Labours of Mrs Stella Ryman: Further Fairmount Mysteries *by Mel Anastasiou* • Trapped in a down-at-the-heels care home. You'd be cranky too. • pulpliterature.com/stella-ryman-and-the-fairmount-manor-mysteries

Paperboy: A Dysfunctional Novel *by Bob Thurber* • Photography by Vincent Louis Carrella • shantiarts.co/uploads/files/thurber_paperboy.html

What the Wind Brings *by Matthew Hughes* • Epic slipstream historical fiction • pulpliterature.com/product-category/novels/matthew-hughes

The Writer's Boon Companion *by Mel Anastasiou* • Thirty Days Towards an Extraordinary Volume • pulpliterature.com/subscribe/the-bookstore

$\mathcal{B}$OOKSTORES

Book Warehouse • 632 Broadway W, Vancouver, BC V5Z 1G1 • 604-872-5711 bookwarehouse.ca

Myth Hawker Travelling Bookstore • Canadian authors • Canadian content • small and independent press • mythhawker.ca

Phoenix On Bowen • 992 Dorman Rd, Bowen Island, BC V0N 1G0 • 604-947-2793

Village Books & Coffee House • 130-12031 First Ave, Richmond, BC V7E 3M1 • 604-272-6601 • villagebooks@shaw.ca

Western Sky Books • 2132-2850 Shaughnessy St, Port Coquitlam, BC V3C 6K5 • 604-461-5602 • store.westernskybooks.com

$\mathcal{C}$ONFERENCES AND EVENTS

SIWC at Sea 2020 • 29 March–25 April 2020 • siwc.ca/siwc-at-sea

Word on the Lake 8–10 May 2020 Salmon Arm, BC wordonthelakewritersfestival.com

Creative Ink Festival • 15–17 May 2020 Burnaby, BC • creativeinkfestival.com

When Words Collide • 14–16 August 2020 Calgary, AB • whenwordscollide.org

Wine Country Writers' Festival 25–26 September 2020 Penticton, BC winecountrywritersfestival.ca

Surrey International Writers' Conference 23–25 October 2020 • Surrey, BC • siwc.ca

NEW FROM
PULP LITERATURE
PRESS

Allaigna's Song Aria

BY JM LANDELS

THE HIGHLY
ANTICIPATED
SEQUEL TO THE
BESTSELLING

Allaigna's Song Overture

You can't escape magic when it's in your blood

pulpliterature.com

Do you have a **story to tell?**
We can help!

Dreamers is dedicated to heartfelt writing. Visit our site for:

- Therapeutic Writing
- Poems & Stories
- Content Marketing
- Creative Nonfiction
- Writing Workshops
- Contests & Anthologies
- Residencies & Retreats
- ...and so much more!

www.DreamersWriting.com

DREAMERS
CREATIVE WRITING

MYTH HAWKER
· TRAVELLING BOOKSTORE ·

"Myth Hawker has a crush on the underdog: the small press, the overlooked author, the independent bookstore, and the vast, undiscovered treasures of small-scale publishing."

Myth Hawker travels the length & breadth of Canada, popping up at conventions & festivals in every province, showcasing the work of small press & independent Canadian authors. Follow them online to see where they're popping up next!

www.mythhawker.com   @Mythhawker

MICHAEL
KAMAKANA
ADVENT
WE THOUGHT WE KNEW WHAT THEY WANTED
WE WERE WRONG

onspec
the canadian magazine   of the fantastic

Expect the unexpected.

www.onspec.ca

The Creative Ink Festival has been postponed. See website for details.

DELTA HOTEL, BURNABY| MAY 15-17, 2020

the Creative Ink

FESTIVAL *for writers & readers*

GoH, Wesley Chu
NY Times Best Selling
Author

GoH Colleen Anderson
3 Time Aurora Nominee

www.creativeinkfestival.com   #CIFest2020

Because every issue is an EVENT.

Read. Subscribe. Submit.

- 2018 Journey Prize Long-list
- 2017 Canadian Magazine Awards Winner,
  Best Literature and Art Story, including Poetry
- 2016 National Magazine Awards Finalist, Fiction
  and Personal Journalism
- 2015 National Magazine Awards Finalist, Poetry

eventmagazine.ca

Combine your love of writing with the beauty and inspiration of the South Okanagan

Art by Rachel Neale

Give me books, [Okanagan] wine, fruit, fine weather and a little music played out of doors by somebody I do not know.
— [almost] **John Keats**

Penticton's **Wine Country Writer's Festival** is a one-day boutique event full of panels, presentations, and personal interactions for writers of all levels

Join us September 25-26, 2020
Penticton Lakeside Resort
WineCountryWritersFestival.ca
WCWF20@gmail.com

only $67 until June 1st
Register now!

BOB THURBER

CONTESTS

Pulp Literature runs four annual contests for poetry, flash fiction, and short stories. For contest guidelines, prizes, and entry fees, see pulpliterature.com/contests.

The Magpie Award for Poetry
Contest opens: 1 March 2020
Deadline: 15 April 2020
Winner notified: 15 May 2020
Winner published: Issue 28, Autumn 2020
Prize: $500

The Hummingbird Flash Fiction Prize
Contest opens: 1 May 2020
Deadline: 15 June 2020
Winner notified: 15 July 2020
Winner published: Issue 29, Winter 2021
Prize: $300

The Raven Short Story Contest
Contest opens: 1 September 2020
Deadline: 15 October 2020
Winner notified: 15 November 2020
Winner published: Issue 30, Spring 2021
Prize: $300

The Bumblebee Flash Fiction Contest

Contest opens: 1 January 2021

Deadline: 15 February 2021

Winner notified: 15 March 2021

Winner published: Issue 31, Summer 2021

Prize: $300

$\mathscr{B}$ECOME A PATRON OF PULP LITERATURE

By supporting *Pulp Literature* on Patreon with $2 or more per month, you will be laying the foundation for a secure future for the magazine, as well as ensuring that you never miss an issue! Your subscription includes four big issues of short stories, novellas, poetry, comics, and novel excerpts, delivered to your door or electronic mailbox each year. **Find us at patreon.com/pulplit**

If you prefer to subscribe through our website, go to pulpliterature.com/subscribe.

Or you can send a cheque with the form below to
Subscriptions, Pulp Literature Press, 21955 16 Ave, Langley BC, V2Z 1K5, Canada

Don't miss an issue!

- ☐ **Send me 2 years (8 issues) at the special rate of $90** (save $30)*
- ☐ **Send me 1 year (4 issues) for $50** (save $10)*
- ☐ **Send me 2 years of digital issues for $30** (save $9.92)
- ☐ **Send me 1 year of digital issues for $17.50** (save $2.47)

Name: ____

Address: ____

City: __________________________________ Prov. / State: __________

Postal code: _______________ Country:___________________________

Email: ____

- ☐ **Payment enclosed**
- ☐ **Bill me**
- ☐ **New**
- ☐ **Renewal**

Make cheques payable in Canadian funds to J. Landels. Include email address for digital editions and Paypal billing, or subscribe at www.pulpliterature.com.

*for postage outside Canada add $20 per year in North America or $36 per year overseas.

www.ingramcontent.com/pod-product-compliance
Lightning Source LLC
Chambersburg PA
CBHW072352220726
48293CB00018B/1089